MW01148228

Balance of Night

Allan P. Avery

a military procedural

Printed by Create Space, an Amazon.com
Company

For Bongo

He flew west too soon.

The duties, demands, and procedures described in this novel are factual within the realm of literary license. The characters and story are fictional and resemblance to real people, living or dead, or to actual events is entirely coincidental. Places and geographical locations are used fictitiously or are fictional. The novel revolves around the routine yet demanding service in a Marine Corps KC-130 Hercules aircraft squadron in what passes for peace time duty. The story is the result of the author's sense of the flavor of the times, experiences and situations that could have evolved into the circumstances told here.

Also by Allan P. Avery

Who Mourns the Egyptian?

Murder in the Florida Panhandle

Printed by Create Space, an Amazon.com Company

Contents

A Note

This novel is a modern military procedural focused on the marines of the Marine Corps KC-130 Hercules squadrons and the aerial refueling mission. People, not automatons, serve in these squadrons, practice and execute the assigned missions. People have professional and personal lives and those lives run in parallel, sometimes cross over, intertwine, and challenge mission dedication. An ability to compartmentalize the professional from the personal is required. This story ranges from the main island of Japan, to Okinawa, Korea, Australia, and points about the Pacific Rim.

The Marine Corps shares a portion of philosophy with the Roman legions of antiquity as stated by Flavius Josephus: "The drills are bloodless battles and the battles are bloody drills." In D.I. parlance, "the more you sweat in peace the less you bleed in war." Some like to dress this up or water it down but in their hearts every marine knows the statement to be true. The marines take pride not in the hard way but, in the right way, because it is the best way which is often the Marine Corps way.

United States Navy, Coast Guard, and Marine Corps pilots are designated Naval Aviators. The flying officers who operate the weapons and sensor systems in multi crew Navy and Marine Corps aircraft such as the F/A-18F Super Hornet are designated Naval Flight Officers. The enlisted marines are designated Air Crew. All are trained to demanding United States Navy standards and all wear wings of gold, Navy wings.

Military pilots and aircrew have or develop an abundance of self confidence. The confidence must be tempered with discipline. Devotion is required to develop the demanding skills associated with flying the aircraft, any aircraft, and, above all, accomplishing the mission.

Chapter One   Night Flight to Kwajalein Atoll

When I lie down, I say, when shall I arise, and the night be gone? And I am full of tossings to and fro unto the dawning of the day.

Job 7:4

A neon yellow meteor tail bright as comic book art slashed the black sky above the Mariana Islands. U.S. Marine Corps Captain Meriwether Lewis Clark MacFarland III, Tumble to his squadron mates, watched the dark tide of night cover the stab of light. Across seven years of service and the seven seas it was the brightest meteor he had seen from the flight deck of the aerial tanker aircraft the KC-130 Hercules.

Tumble pulled a yellow bag of peanut and chocolate candy, from the lower left pocket of his Nomex olive drab flight suit. He transferred the bag to his right hand and held it above the throttle quadrant on the center console.

"Pogey bait?" he said.

Without a word Gunnery Sergeant Rodeo Simpson, the flight engineer, took a dozen pieces. The gunny sat just aft of the center console and minded the store from there.

"Only if it is peanut and chocolate," said First Lieutenant Bongo Markam the second pilot or T2P.

"Your lucky day," said Tumble.

The startling show of color from the meteor and the conversation stirred the men on the flight deck. Now, each commented or shifted position or coughed.

The KC-130 Hercules, the Herc, had departed Marine Corps Air Station (MCAS) Sakura, Japan in dreary weather. Full darkness, early in accordance with the season, had come in the late afternoon. The lousy weather was accompanied by high winds at altitude. The night flight was for celestial navigation proficiency.

The mission was a combination of training and approved boondoggle. The eventual destination was Brisbane, Australia for Christmas week. The plan was to log pilot night time on a dog leg celestial navigation route to Kwajalien Atoll in the Marshall Islands. Celestial navigation was a dying art and this would be among the last official proficiency missions. CWO-4 Low Rent Wojecki was the navigator; one of the last and best of a fading breed. The J model Hercules was coming.

Newer, faster, and probably better it was reluctantly admitted after the third beer. Automation would replace the navigator and change the function and title of other crewmembers. However, for now, Tumble was satisfied with the Hamilton Standard prop beat.

Low Rent Wojecki stood behind Gunny Rodeo Simpson. He cracked and peeled a boiled egg from his box lunch. He admired the naked egg as if a Faberge then took the peeled egg and held it against the sextant port. He used his off hand to flip the sextant port open. The pressure differential shot the egg up the chute and out into the night.

"When I was a corporal I thought that was the neatest trick," said Rent.

"Hard to give up the old ways," said Rodeo. He and Rent had flown together since both were corporals.

Rent ignored him and poked the barrel of the periscopic sextant into the open port for a three star shot. A good three star fix was necessary and the requirement pleased Rent. The single inertial navigation system had gone tango uniform, tits up, fifteen minutes after takeoff. The last two fixes had indicated the jet stream had dropped down in both latitude and altitude, not unusual in the winter months, but over 150 knots of quartering tailwind gave them a very high ground speed, for a Herc, and required a high angle of westerly crab to maintain course. The flight would be quicker than expected but the crab into the wind had to be maintained or they could go Earhart. No one even considered turning around. Marines had been crossing the Pacific, by the stars, before these marines had been born. Besides, Christmas in Brisbane, they would make it if they had to flap their arms.

A designated Marine navigator was good at his job as no other kind was designated. Using a sextant and an Air Almanac the navigator would find the island speck called Kwaj and Australia would be a given.

The trip was a good deal and Tumble had received it by default. The squadron commanding officer Lieutenant Colonel Wild Bill Hitchcock had slated himself for it. Wild Bill had come down with mono and, at the last moment, had grudgingly taken himself off the flight. It was a Saturday and Tumble had been in the squadron area at MCAS Naha, Okinawa for a maintenance hop. The one time "you're the only one available" had worked in his favor. The duty S-1 corporal had cut his orders while he hurried back to the BOQ for a bag drag. Then he and the crew had flown the Herc up to MCAS Sakura on Honshu, the main island of Japan, for the passenger pickup. There would be a stutter step day on Kwaj while his name was added to the diplomatic clearance request. The crew would use the layover day to fly a low level training mission through the Marshall and Gilbert Islands. The day after that the flight would continue south across the Solomon Islands and the Coral Sea to Brisbane. Male or female the dreams of a marine on liberty could come true.

Locked down in the back of the Herc was a 3,600 gallon aluminum, beer can shaped, fuselage fuel tank accompanied by thirty deserving marines on Christmas leave. The marines were chosen from outstanding performers from the ranks of private through sergeant and came from Okinawa and main land Japan. Each marine was carrying leave papers and $500 cash for expenses. Even a good marine might fib on his ATM account. Bongo and the loadmaster, Sergeant Hostile Lopez, had personally sighted these two items plus a military identification card for each manifested marine. This was not to prevent an unauthorized marine from boarding but to ensure the minimum items were in possession of each marine.

Cruising at twenty-five thousand feet the Herc was five thousand feet above a thick and solid cloud layer. An occasional cumulonimbus reared an ugly hammerhead plume to ten thousand feet above the Herc and spit lightning from cloud to cloud and across the cloud. The radar required attention and was used to make weather avoidance turns. Starlight punctuated the night sky above. Lights from the islands, and ships, and fishing boats below did not penetrate the great layers of cloud and rain. They flew to give the buildups wide berth but the air was rough and bounced the Herc about. Rodeo Simpson kept the back of the Herc uncomfortably cold in an effort to keep the passengers from getting air sick.

Navy Lieutenant Juan Talliaferro, Don Juan, the squadron flight surgeon, stood behind Bongo. He peered west, beyond the small glow of cockpit lighting and into the balance of night.

"Our chance to be famous, boys," Juan said.

"Don Juan you are infamous," said Tumble.

"You are referring to my pro bono holistic approach to tactile mammography?"

"You are the reason I am considering medical school," said Bongo.

"Not the same is it Juan?" Rent said as he turned to plot his three star fix at the navigator station right side aft in the cockpit.

"The difference is if the national news carries your story at 6:30 pm or you are on the 7 pm with the questioning minds and paparazzi. Probably the 7 pm. We have an unidentified flying object closing from 2 o'clock and slightly low," said Juan. He did not take his eyes from the window.

Bongo spit tobacco into his white foam cup and twisted in his seat to look over his right shoulder.

"It won't be unidentified for long, Tumble. It's closing. Looks like a formation join up. Hope they know what they're doing."

"I hope they see us," said Tumble.

In the back of the Hercules the lights were low and the temperature cold. Some of the thirty marines were lying on thin red sling seats similar to lawn furniture. The seats were positioned longitudinally down each side of the fuselage. Other marines were sprawled on the theoretically heated cargo deck. Sugar plums and other Australian fantasies danced in their dreams. They were oblivious to all external to their immediate and uncomfortable world.

Their friends and some who were not their friends called them Spider and Dirt. The nicknames or call signs, allowed approved familiarity, speed of communication, and unofficial code. The personal call signs made life a little more livable aboard an aircraft carrier. Now, each would be called scared. Dirt would prefer the word worried but it was a big and aggressive worry. Spider did not have the leisure to consider the difference.

They had launched from the starboard bow catapult of the aircraft carrier USS Bobby Lee. They were from VF-Double Trouble and flying the two-seat F/A-18F Super Hornet fighter aircraft. It was a great jet but a notorious fuel boozer when it was dark outside and it was very dark out there.

Now, the jet was so low on JP-5 jet fuel it was no longer worth mentioning. A miracle was called for; a break in the undercast would do. They would not have to eject into a void, blindly swing under their parachutes and drift through black and turbulent and billowing cumulonimbus clouds into the big and lonely Pacific.

The Bobby Lee was an older carrier but age, in any port, had never mattered to Spider. Perhaps the fates owed him a break and Bobby would appear below them. They could make a low fuel carrier landing. Even if their fuel was exhausted they could punch out in sight of the big gray boat. The angel, a rescue helicopter, would scoop them out of the water using a fearless twenty year old rescue swimmer. Boat, it was a derisive term to the black shoes, the surface Navy, and therefore dear to the hearts of the brown shoes, the aviators.

Normally, the fighter would not have been alone but the wingman had gone down for a last second maintenance problem on the port catapult. Too bad, on the cat stroke, 0 to 150 knots in four heart beats, their communications and navigation gear had gone blank. In theory it should not happen but that was why it was called a theory. This was particularly embarrassing to Dirt as he was the avionics officer and it was his gear that was no longer working. Fortunately, the standby primary flight instruments of gyro, airspeed, vertical speed, compass and needle and ball worked as designed. The prime directive in the airplane business is to aviate and that was what Spider was doing. The navigate and communicate parts were problems but the jet was blue side up.

Airborne off the catapult Spider and Dirt had penetrated a 400 feet overcast and committed for the operational cycle. No big deal was the initial thought. They had plenty of gas. The recoveries would not start until the launch was complete. They would hang out on top and sooner or later join on another Double Trouble bubba. It would be a great ready room story and worth beers at the Officers Club.

They had broken through the tops at twenty thousand feet and waited. The intercom system worked and Spider had not passed up the chance to harangue the avionics division officer in the back seat. Soon, there was a bit of apprehension. No other aircraft appeared on top. No blinking red anti-collision lights, or strobes, or green and red position lights, ghostly green formation lights. The launch cycle must have stopped after their catapult shot. It was unusual but not unheard. The weather was bad but something else must have happened. Maybe a jet lost off the cat or a tug driven into a parked aircraft on the deck or a sailor thrown into the sea from the plunging deck. They just had to wait while all was sorted out and the Bobby Lee figured out the launched jet had lost communication and navigation and that what could not happen had happened.

Dirt continuously tried the radios and checked circuit breakers. There was no indication of transmission out or in, no side tones. On the off chance it was his radio controls or helmet he asked Spider to make a transmission. No one answered. Dirt took the radio from his survival vest and transmitted. He heard the side tones but no joy, no answer. The range was limited on the survival radios. He decided to save his battery and went to a listening watch. Still, help would arrive soon and when the other jet appeared it would be close enough for the use of the survival radio, so not too bad. Dirt looked out of the cockpit. It was night; they were above the Pacific Ocean and south of the Tropic of Cancer. Seasonal thunderstorms and general bad weather covered the ocean. There was not a speck of light penetrating from below. Dirt laughed aloud to bolster his courage and dug in the left shoulder pocket of his flight suit for his snuff can.

The night did not bother Spider. It was the darkness. No communication plus no navigation gave an unusual sum for the Hornet.

Company would be nice. Another jet along side; they would tag along and go back to the big gray boat. Make a formation approach in the goo and get dropped off on the ball.

"Bingo profile?" Dirt said.

"Thinking," said Spider.

Dirt had a point. Go high and save gas. Save gas to go where? No one was looking for them high. Descend through the clouds and count on seeing the ocean at night below the 400 feet cloud base. What kind of horizon would he have there? If he was within a mile of the ship could he spot it at 400 feet altitude? Was the ceiling still that high? The Hornet used gas very fast down low. Was the transponder working? Squawk emergency 7700 then lost communications 7600 anyway. If the transponder was working it would confirm to the Bobby Lee what it had already figured. Go lower spot a sucker hole and go for it? While he thought the situation over Spider slowed to his best fuel conserving speed for the altitude. Winds, what were the winds doing to them? There was a big jet stream swooping down and the bucking jet told him they were nibbling at it. It was hard to tell. He should have paid more attention to the weather brief. After college he should have stayed in Vidalia and gone into the insurance business with Billie's Dad. Sold life insurance and car policies to the onion farmers; married Billie, had three kids, gone to church every Sunday. He would have made a lot of money for that part of the country. Played golf, didn't like golf. Was that why he had punched? Nope, he wanted adventure; the kind that gets a small town boy out of the small town. The adventure the sailor in blue on the recruiting poster outside the post office promised. The adventure part seemed to be working out. The lost at sea part had not been mentioned on the poster. The phrase "lost at sea" had finality about it.

Airborne eighty minutes and Dirt had monitored his survival radio without hearing a thing. He had transmitted in the blind but was conscious of the radio's limited battery power. No telling how much he might need the radio floating in a one man raft. He continually rotated his head and looked about. Finally, he saw a blink of light and pulled his survival radio out of his vest, turned the volume full up and listened. No need to transmit yet. Conserve the battery. The boys were here and looking for them. Maybe it was a Hornet with a buddy store and bringing them a little gas for a night air refueling, very nice.

"Spider, check 9 o'clock low. Rotating beacon."

"Got it. Going for it."

"Don't over run."

"Buy you beer for a week if I do."

"Buy you beer for a month if you don't."

They closed and it became obvious the other aircraft was slower and bigger and it was all Spider could do at idle and boards to keep from overshooting on the join up.

The silhouette of the C-130 Hercules is unique and recognizable worldwide to those who have educated themselves in aircraft identification.

"Herc. How much longer do you think we can stay in the air?" said Dirt.

"Twenty-five plus or minus."

"U.S. Herc?"

"Let's see."

"Partner," Dirt said. "The way I see it is we come up beside the transport puke, get his attention. When we come to the moment we eject. Even a transport pilot will see two rocket seats firing in his face. Climb in our rafts when we get to the water and wait. This guy can call someone to come get us. He'll be a hero."

"Get an air medal for rescuing us."

"Better for the C.O. to ask why we punched and not ask why we didn't."

"Better to be judged by six at the Field Flight Performance Board than carried by six. Break out your survival radio. Give them a call on guard, 243zip."

Inside the Herc all eyes were watching the closing aircraft lights. As required they were monitoring the UHF radio emergency guard frequency 243 mhz.

"Bongo, make a who goes call on guard," said Tumble.

Bongo could see the lights of the closing aircraft, almost make out the silhouette. Before he could transmit he heard a radio call.

"Hey, Herc. You have a Hornet coming close on your starboard. Do you hear me?"

"Dirt, Dirt."

"Spider, this guy knows my name."

"What? No. That's me."

"Knock it off Spider. I'm trying to make sure this guy sees us. If he had good eyes he'd be in fighters."

"Dirt, it's a tanker, a Marine KC, a flying gas station."

"Hail Mary full of grace," Dirt said aloud then transmitted on the handheld survival radio.

"Texaco, Texaco, Texaco. Emergency fuel Hornet on your starboard side and we need gas now."

"Gunny, get the hoses out and the observers up. We have a customer and he's in a hurry," said Tumble.

Gunny Rodeo Simpson did not clutter the primary intercom as he let his flying hands answer the aircraft commander. He called the observers to their stations at the rear paratroop door windows on a second intercom circuit.

Bongo selected Guard for transmission on his radio control panel.

"We got you partner. Stay clear, eighty feet and fifteen hundred pounds of refueling hose coming out each side. Give us two minutes."

"That's all we've got."

"Which side do you want?"

"The closest."

"Roger. Check switches safe, nose cold. You're cleared to plug. It'll be a wet one from the start."

Dirt watched as Spider extended the refueling probe from the Hornet's shoulder. Dirt did not want a fuel check. It was what it was. He cinched his seat straps tighter and tugged at the Koch fittings. If they had to leave suddenly he wanted to be snug when he slapped into a 250 knot airstream.

Spider was focused. He ignored the big Herc tail and fuselage abeam his port wing. He was where he should be and that was half the battle. He was not the pilot because he was not apart from the machine. He was cyborg. He was the jet and the jet was ready. His eyes saw what needed to be seen. His hands and feet made the myriad minor adjustments on throttles and flight controls that were required to maneuver into position. It was like caressing a wife of twenty years. You knew where everything was and where you should go and a lot of trouble was avoided if you did it right from the start.

The jet formed a bow wave of air as a boat forms a bow wave of water. Spider was prepared when the tumbling air rolled over and nudged and bounced the refueling basket. He shoved the extended Hornet refueling probe through the stabilizing vanes, the turkey feathers, about the knuckle of the fueling receptacle. The force of the closure rate was sufficient to tap the ball valves, push them back, and allow fuel to flow. The Hornet was now attached to the Herc by 1500 pounds and eighty feet of refueling hose which was now pushed back on the reel and seventy feet separated the nose of the Hornet from the refueling pod under the outboard portion of the Herc wing. The port side distance to the Herc was less than that. Spider ignored the nearness of the other aircraft. They maintained their relative positions. He glanced at the end of the refueling pod. He saw the green fuel flow light and that was a good thing.

Dirt held his breath. He did not speak encouraging words.

The Hornet lurched right and dropped down separating from the refueling basket.

"Flame out on two. One is good. Trust me."

"You the man, Spider."

The starboard observer in the Herc was a 19 year old lance corporal attending to his appointed duty. He pressed his intercom switch and said, "The Hornet fell out of the basket."

Across the radio came another weak transmission.

"We have lost number two to fuel starvation."

In the cockpit Tumble lowered the Herc's nose a degree or less and decreased the power to maintain constant airspeed in the descent.

"Tell them we'll toboggan. Start downhill at two hundred feet a minute and more if needed. They're coasting."

Bongo transmitted. It was more encouragement than instruction. The bubbas would fly formation no matter the attitude and they would recognize the opportunity for a single engine second plug.

Spider shook his head and refocused. Later, over beers, he would say it was like the time he caught his one high school touchdown pass against arch rival Lyons. The only thing he saw was the ball. He maneuvered the jet with the starboard engine flamed out and wind-milling. He inserted the refueling probe and gave the number one throttle an ever so slight bump to ensure sufficient closure to push in the refueling hose and start the fuel flowing again.

The port side number one engine RPM began to decrease. A bad thing in a two-engine jet with one engine already stopped.

"Dirt, we're losing one. We may have to give the jet back to the tax payers."

"Fuel flow," Rodeo Simpson said over the cockpit intercom.

"Green light, fuel flow," Bongo transmitted.

"Give us a better descent rate. We're losing the other engine. Going for the relight."

"You got it," said Bongo. He looked left at Tumble.

Tumble nodded, said nothing and dropped the nose to about three degrees below the gyroscopic horizon and picked up a 700 feet per minute rate of descent and twenty knots. It was faster than the "suppose to go" speed for the Herc but the Hornet was gravity powered.

Flame shot from the number one Hornet engine.

"Relight observed," said the observer.

"We got 'em, Dirt. We've got both of them. Tell Texaco to keep it coming."

"I hate it when you show off," said Dirt.

The two plane formation was now a night instrument formation as they entered the cloud tops at 270 knots.

"Bongo, we need to level and slow about 20 knots. Con su permiso the suck and blow bubba."

"Okay. He'll have to be ahead on fuel."

Bongo made the transmission.

"Tell him we're good for that and keep the gas coming. We'll stay with him. Ask him where we are going," said Spider.

"Okay. Hope the battery in this PRC radio will last a while longer," answered Dirt.

"Me too; we're in the soup by the way.

"Yeah; I'm afraid to look outside."

"Rodeo, how's our fuel?" said Tumble.

"Fifteen thousand, sir," said Rodeo.

"Bongo, give him an ETA for Kwaj. Ask him how much fuel he needs including approach and landing."

Bongo asked the question. Then repeated the answer they received.

"Six maybe, eight no problem. Radios and navaids are gone. He's transmitting on the radio from his survival vest.

"Weather report from Kwaj, sir," said Sergeant Hostile Lopez from his radio operator and load master flight deck position.

"Go."

"Five hundred foot ceiling, one mile visibility, ten knots of wind down the runway."

"He doesn't want to land with zero. We're already giving away our island holding fuel. Should have bagged it out on gas. All those staff guys strapped to their desks and pushing fiscal efficiency and eco flying aren't sitting here, at night, middle of the ocean and alligators snapping. We'll make two approaches. A formation approach, drop him off and come back around. I want to drop him off and have no less than six so we'll be on the ground with 4 point 5. If we had to we could give a heart beat delay after the drop," said Tumble.

"We give him maybe 5,000 and make two approaches and he'll land with little and we'll be a long way into our backup gas. Closer to 3 than 4 point 5 on the deck," said Bongo.

"Best we can do. We have thirty marines in the back and we'll be out of gas and ideas at the same time."

"Never met a fighter pilot I couldn't learn to dislike."

"Know what you mean, Bongo. Give them the scoop. Tell them to stay close. We'll give them the gas."

Chapter Two Kwajalein

Bongo looked ahead into the dark, engulfing, suspended moisture. The Herc bucked with the turbulence. He sipped the dregs of bad coffee and keyed the radio.

"Are you boys VFW members?" Bongo said.

"Not yet," said Dirt.

"Nice one at Kwajalein. We can probably get you in. That's where we are going."

"Okay. We're talking on the pricks, survival radios. Don't know how much longer the batteries will last."

"Not a problem."

"Not for you."

"Just stay with us. When we start the approach get on the starboard side, formation approach and dirty when we dirty. We'll take you down and drop you off. Go to a listening watch. We'll use light signals. Unless you have to transmit use your flashlight to answer. One blink is yes and two is no."

"Sir, I've got one flashlight blink from the receiver aircraft," said the lance corporal observer.

"He passes the IQ test," said Juan.

Dirt and Spider were pleased to be dry. They were not ecstatic. It was dark and turbulent. They were low fuel and twenty-thousand feet was not an efficient cruise altitude for a Hornet and 250 knots was not a favorite speed. They compared the information passed to them by the tanker with their fuel consumption versus the fuel on board. It was enough for one pass at the deck and a zoom climb with a pop at the top if they did not make the landing.

"Spider, this is a lot riding on the wing of a transport pilot."

"Yeah, if he was any good he would be flying fighters."

"You said that already. Don't say it to him."

"Just making conversation."

"Sir," said Sergeant Lopez, "I have passed the situation to Kwaj on the high freq. Their search and rescue uses a boat. They are alerting the crew. We are the only aircraft inbound and they'll be ready for us. An aircraft carrier, the Bobby Lee, is looking for a jet. I told them we found one and Kwaj is passing the word."

"Thanks," said Tumble.

"Wonder how that happened? Somebody is searching for a story right now," said Bongo.

Fifteen minutes later Bongo was able to talk to Kwajalein on the UHF radio. In another fifteen they would be at the start descent point. The yellow-green to blue-green filigreed web of St. Elmo's fire played about the cockpit windows and all about lightning periodically split the darkness. The yellow and blue flashes silhouetted towering cumulonimbus clouds marking the huge Pacific Ocean thunderstorms.

"How are we doing on fuel?" Tumble said.

"Nine thousand, sir," said Rodeo.

"Put the hoses back out. Bongo, wake the bubbas. Tell them fifteen hundred pounds coming their way."

"I've never met a fighter pilot that, given time, I could not learn to dislike."

"Same song, second verse. Give them the gas. It's tough growing up not knowing who your father is."

Bongo put the yellow bag of chocolate covered, peanut candies on the center console, pulled out a can of snuff; put a fresh pinch behind his lower lip.

"How about a cup of coffee?" he said and then cleared the Hornet in for more.

"If he had extra why didn't he give it to us before?" Dirt said as he acknowledged the tanker with a single flashlight blink.

Spider wanted to drink water. He could smell the worry in his perspiration. The sweat soaked his flight suit. Gradually, he had become aware of the hum and chatter of small vibrations in the cockpit, the noise of air passing the canopy and, most of all, the odor of old sweat from the men before him. The sweat had rolled from their bodies during countless high G maneuvers and night carrier landings. Now, his body heat was reviving the scent. He was aware of the cold. He was very cold now. He was freezing and sweating at the same time. Dehydration would soon become a factor.

"It is not extra gas, Dirt. This is his. He is sharing. It takes gas to carry gas. He has done us a favor."

"Please and thank you. I'll mind my manners."

"Wish I had gone to confession Sunday."

"I thought you were Baptist; not Catholic."

"What is your point?"

"Let's do it."

No wasted motion or energy. Spider extended the refueling probe and put it in the basket. Green light and the JP-5 flowed through the seventy feet of hose separating him from the Herc. His fuel quantity gages confirmed the jet fuel splashing into his tanks. It was not much but it was enough to keep the Hornet flying and that was the most important goal in the world to the two men strapped into their respective portion of cockpit.

"Tumble, I'm looking over the approach plate. Buckholtz Field at Kwaj and the best there is a non-precision tacan approach. (A non-precision approach provides course guidance without glide slope information). Minimum descent altitude is four-hundred feet. It was okay when we had two hours island holding fuel because this weather will move on by. We're a bit scochi now," Bongo said using the Americanized version of the Japanese word for a little bit. He spit snuff into a white foam cup.

"I know. The final approach course is over water. We'll nail the course and take her down to the MDA. If we have to we'll go past that on the radar altimeter, hundred foot limit. The fighter will be on our wing, stepped up a hair. I don't want to peel him off on the water. If he is stepped down that could happen. He'll know what we have to do but brief him anyway. Eliminate confusion. I'll fly and you call the runway in sight on the guard frequency. We may have to touch and go as we drop him off. He'll land straight ahead. We will come back around for our own approach and landing. It will be right the first time. Check for arresting gear and pass him the runway length."

"Sounds like a plan to me. No arresting gear listed," said Bongo.

"The storm cells seem to be moving away from the field. We aren't going to get a better chance," said Rent.

"Bongo, tell Kwaj control we are commencing. We'll make a continuous, steady rate descent. Save a couple of pounds on fuel. Tell the boys following us we're on the way to the house. We'll call dirty on the numbers. We'll fly the final approach segment at 135 knots with fifty flaps. Don't know what the Hornet approach speed is. Not right then he'll speak up. I've never seen a fighter pilot who wasn't a good formation pilot so hanging with us won't be a problem."

There was silence on the flight deck. Rodeo looked at the fuel gages. No surprises. No news.

Hostile checked the pax. Most were sleeping. He reached down into the right calf pocket of his flight suit and grabbed his worry beads. He began to run the beads between thumb and fore finger.

Bongo picked up his new cup of old coffee, drank it past the snuff and then gave the approach brief to the fighter crew.

"We got one flashlight blink back here," said the lance corporal.

Tumble had been in the bounce pattern with Hornets. The speeds had been compatible. The fighter boys were not transmitting so all was okay. He drove the Hercules deeper into the darkness. It was solid black outside. There was no longer starlight to silhouette the bulging cloud tops. His peripheral vision no longer noted the intimidating appearance of the thunder clouds. Updrafts shook the Herc. The interior was cold.

Rodeo had Hostile double check the pax. He selected manual and ran warmer air into the cockpit. He left the temperature cold in the back. He did not want thirty marines sick in the back of his airplane.

Tumble's eyes absorbed the vital available information: course alignment, airspeed, rate of descent, altitude, and attitude. The flight instruments provided the raw data and his trained brain transformed the data into a three dimensional moving diagram. It was as autonomous as breathing. He controlled his aircraft, now weighing less than one-hundred thousand pounds, by gentle pressures and slight movements.

Tumble wanted a stable set up for the long, straight-in approach. He decided on a generous mile in level flight prior to the final approach fix, the point where he would start the final descent for landing. The level flight would cost a few pounds of precious fuel and if he were a single ship he would have done it differently but he had a jet without approach capability on his wing and the payoff would be an increased chance of getting it right the first time.

Level at fifteen hundred feet above the unseen ocean; slowing past one-hundred eighty knots, almost two-hundred miles per hour across the ground, Tumble called for fifty percent flaps. The big fowler flaps moved aft and downwards increasing the chord width of the Herc wing, increasing drag and lift and lowering the stall speed. Tumble led the flaps with elevator pressure and trim as the Herc tried to balloon up with the new lift. A mile prior to the final approach fix Tumble called, "gear down, landing checklist," as Kwajalein Control cleared them to land.

Tumble had the Herc at 135 knots indicated air speed, a ballpark Herc approach speed for most weights, at the final approach fix located five miles from the end of the 6,673 feet long runway 6 at Buckholtz Field, Kwajalein, Marshall Islands. He retarded the four throttles two knob widths and dropped the Herc nose three degrees. When the vertical speed indicator showed downward motion he tweaked the nose up by half, adjusted power and trim and stabilized at 135 knots and a max thousand feet per minute rate of descent. At five-hundred feet above the published minimum descent altitude of 420 feet he decreased the rate of descent and adjusted the throttles and trim. He leveled the Herc at the MDA. The instrument indicated distance to the runway steadily decreased. They were still short of the missed approach point which was over the tacan located next to the runway. It was the position he wanted. His eyes did not stray from the flight instruments. Rodeo watched the aircraft systems and Bongo strained his eyes for the sight of the runway lights or the sea.

"Nothing," said Bongo at two miles to go.

The rain appeared as horizontal strands through the illumination from the nose wheel lights and wing lights as it beat against the windscreen. In the cockpit the noise of each rain drop against the aircraft seemed as distinct as a ball peen hammer strike.

"Roger," Tumble said. He began a very shallow rate of descent cross checking his barometric altimeter and radar altimeter in addition to course, speed, and attitude. He passed the forbidden veil to consciously descend below the minimum descent altitude. The choices were limited.

"White caps, white caps, level off," said Bongo.

"Leveling two-hundred feet," said Tumble. "The fighter is stepped up a hair. Don't know what he sees. Confirm landing checks at fifty flaps. We'll touch and go for the drop."

"Landing checks reviewed complete," said Bongo.

The Kwajalein approach light system is almost non-existent. It has a two-bar visual approach slope indicator and white runway side lights.

"Runway. Twelve o'clock. VASI in sight. Keep it coming," said Bongo.

Tumble was soaked with sweat; his eyes felt as if they had been sanded with fine grit sandpaper. His shoulders ached from the constant muscular tension. He knew he was gripping the control yoke too tight for best technique. He forced himself to loosen his grip and went to finger tips on the horns of the yoke. He flicked his eyes up without moving his head. A quick head movement could induce vertigo. There, he saw the VASI. It was red over red. They were too low. Red over red and you're dead, red over white and you're alright. It was Pensacola basics.

He leveled the Herc to drive onto the VASI glide-path from underneath, a dicey technique. He could not risk the climb back to the glide path for fear of losing the runway in close. The VASI lights changed color from red to pink and then separated red over white as the Herc hit the three degree glide slope point. During an approach power is altitude and attitude is airspeed. He eased the throttles back a knob width to reduce the power, dropped the nose a hair and trimmed. The big Herc began to descend and the airspeed remained constant.

"I have the runway, standby for a touch and go. I'll off set left and give them the center," said Tumble.

Tumble eased the control yoke back and flared the Herc. He felt the main landing gear touch the runway. He called, "flaps check set fifty." He pushed all four throttles forward and felt the power surge from the Allison T-56 engines driving the four bladed Hamilton Standard propellers as they gouged huge chunks of air, threw it past the wide straight wings, accelerated the Hercules and lifted it back into the air.

The right observer, from the aft paratroop door window, confirmed the Hornet was on the runway. They were back into the goo before their landing gear was up.

The drop off from the Herc was perfect. The centerline of the runway lined up between Spider's legs. He had a heart beat to check the situation before the Hornet touched down. Rain water flew up in twin rooster tails from the landing gear and melded into one large spray as it flew into the merging engine exhaust pattern. Rain formed a continuous sheet of water flowing from the two-hundred feet wide runway and the runway was slick. Spider worked the brakes carefully, attentively. He had dropped the tail hook when he lowered the landing gear. The Herc boys had said there was not an arresting gear but they could be wrong and he did not want to dribble past a big arresting cable because a transport pilot misread an airport diagram. Stopping was not at the top of the list for an otherwise wonderful airplane. A dozen quick heart beats and he could tell the Hornet was slowing. He brought it to a full stop and looked about. He could see the end of the runway ahead and maybe the white caps of breakers beyond that. It began to rain harder.

"Spider, let's clear the runway. That low fuel Herc is headed back here. I see a follow me truck to the left," said Dirt.

Spider turned his head one-hundred twenty degrees left and saw a yellow rotating light atop a pickup truck. He started the Hornet forward then pushed the left rudder pedal, nose wheel steering engaged, and made a sharp, low speed left turn.

The truck led them onto an expanse of concrete. A man dressed in a yellow rain suit jumped out of the passenger side of the truck and raised both hands. Each hand held a flashlight with orange plastic cones attached. The taxi director raised and lowered the flashlights from waist height to over his head, extended his arms straight out from his shoulders and then slowly raised them over his head until the lights came together, the stop signal.

Spider set his brakes and, thumbs pointed inboard, hand signaled for chocks. The truck driver set the chocks; came out from under the wings and held his extended thumbs inboard in front of his chest. The chocks were in. Spider checked his ejection seat safety pins in place, confirmed the same for Dirt. He saw external power was connected to the jet. The rain was beating down but when would it stop? He opened the canopy and shut down both engines. They climbed out of the jet and closed the canopy as quick as they could.

Spider took a deep breath. The rain rolled off his helmet and into the oxygen mask that hung from one side. The air provided the taste of sea, damp sand, and lingering jet fuel exhaust. He appreciated all of it.

"We owe those guys beers," said Dirt.

"Proud to buy all they want," said Spider.

"Missed approach checklist and fuel check," said Tumble.

Bongo ran the checks.

"Three thousand pounds," said Rodeo.

Theoretically, three thousand was a rough half hour of flying. The last three thousand pounds was a different story. Some fuel was not available at anytime. It was trapped fuel. Some fuel was available part of the time and depended on the aircraft attitude and some fuel would be available all the time up to the gone point. This was not to mention no one trusted Herc fuel gages when they indicated below a thousand pounds in a tank.

"All cross feeds open, Gunny?"

"Been open, sir. All fuel pumps on."

"We will be in the chocks in fifteen minutes with gas to spare," said Bongo.

Tumble glanced at Bongo. It was what the crew needed to hear.

"We're reversing course back to the tacan at fifteen hundred feet, teardrop entry for the final approach course. We'll dirty procedure turn inbound. One hundred flap landing," said Tumble.

"Sounds good," said Bongo.

"Right behind you," said Rodeo. It was an old joke.

No other comments came across the intercom system. Tumble knew every crewmember was listening. He gave a quick thought to the thirty marine passengers. Had anyone had the time to brief them? Well, they were marines and marines don't leave their dead and damn sure not their living.

Either there was enough fuel or there was not. Further short cuts on the actual instrument approach would decrease the odds of a successful outcome. They broke out, runway in sight, a heartbeat before touchdown. Tumble put the KC-130 down firmly and reversed the four Hamilton Standard propellers, each 13.5 feet tip to tip, and attached to T-56 -A-16 Allison engines. The Herc hit a wall of its own making as the prop blade angle went barn door flat; then reverse and the Herc was slowed to a walking pace. Taxiing onto the ramp Rodeo brought the engines to ground RPMs and shut down the two outboard engines while starting the APU, auxiliary power unit, for ground power. They parked next to the Kwaj VFW club house.

Chapter Three Club Rules

Spider and Dirt stood on the wet, sparse grass and coarse damp sand at the edge of the dimly lit ramp. The rain had softened and plastered their hair, soaked their flight suits, and huge water drops dripped from the tip of Dirt's hawk nose. They had teeth baring smiles on their faces and a case of beer under their left arms; open beers were in their right hands. Four men from the VFW braved the drizzle with them while another half dozen peered through the picture window of the squat, concrete block clubhouse.

The men in the VFW were contract employees on the down range end of the Pacific Missile Test Range. The range started at Vandenberg Air Force Base, over four thousand nautical miles away, in California.

A man wearing a blue white lettered "Save the Merchant Fleet" ball cap led the group to the Herc as the propellers stopped. A bit of fuel dribbled from the drain mast under each engine nacelle. The crew entrance door, front left side of the Herc, opened. The waiting group gave a ragged cheer.

Hostile Lopez looked out the door and then called up to the flight deck, "Captain, you need to see this."

Tumble made his way down the ladder from the flight deck, peeked out and then emerged. A wet man grabbed his hand and another pounded him on the back.

Someone gave him a bear hug. Out of the left corner of his vision Tumble saw a case of beer fall to the ramp. He heard a crash and pop, saw cans of beer explode and spew foam and beer chest high. Tumble's feet left the ground. There was cheering and shouting. He was a prisoner on a pogo stick.

His feet back on the ground Tumble recognized the two Navy aviators by their flight suits. One was an easy six feet three inches tall and well over two hundred pounds. The other had the red hair and freckles of a storybook Irishman.

The big one grabbed Tumble's hand and pumped it like he had to water the livestock and said, "Thanks. You and your crew, thank you."

The red head gave Tumble a two handed shake. The royal blue name tag on his flight suit was embroidered on three lines with gold thread Naval Aviator wings top, Spider center, and VF Double Trouble last. The man was near speechless; the relief was in his eyes along with a glint of tear or rain or both.

"Good job, fine job, exceptional job, thanks," said Spider.

The ball cap wearing man made introductions none would remember but it made all of them part of the event.

Another shout from the delegation and Tumble knew the remainder of the crew was coming out. Spider and Dirt began to hand out beers. Froth and foam spewed from the cans. Dirt poured beer on those around him. No one minded. It was good to be alive.

Tumble held his beer, stood his ground. He wanted to sit. No time for that.

"Thanks for the beer," he said. "We have to put this airplane to bed and there are thirty marines in the back to get to quarters."

"Party first," said Dirt.

"You are all invited to the VFW. Crew and passengers," said the man wearing the ball cap.

"Your money is no good in there," Spider said. "We will buy the place if we have to."

"They could use a juke box and a beer or soda and maybe the passengers more than anyone. It was not the ride they expected."

The external power cart connected to the Herc rumbled in the back ground and the self clearing APU was shut down.

"Bongo, have Gunny Simpson fall the marines in under the wing."

The marines stood in three ranks, not really out of the rain but it was the best that could be done and they were use to that. The temp was cool for Kwaj, maybe 75 degrees F. The area was lit by the glow through the VFW window, the vertical light shaft from the Herc retracted wing landing light, and a couple of pole lights. The rain became a mist. The ramp had a sleek sheen to it with an occasional puddle containing a rainbow made by a prism of waste oil. No breeze stirred but the wet scents of sea, sand, old burned jet fuel, and palms hung in the air. The coconut palms seemed to bend toward the formation in an effort to hear.

"Marines, ten-hut and listen up," said Gunny Simpson. He eyed the formation for correctness and numbers, placed his right toe behind his left heel, pivoted his body one hundred eighty degrees on left heel and ball of right foot and faced Tumble in the position of attention. He wanted to show the sand crabs and penguins, the civilians and sailors, how marines did it. He saluted and said, "All present, sir."

"Thank you, Gunny," said Tumble. He returned the salute.

Gunny Simpson made a left face, stepped off to a right face, took three steps and did another about face to offset himself behind Tumble.

"At ease," said Tumble.

The marines relaxed. Some stood with a salty slouch but all were silent and expectant.

"Marines, tonight you went in harm's way. We saved a Navy fighter and the lives of the two crewmembers. You can be proud. You did your duty. You maintained your personal discipline. I want to thank you as do the men you saved."

Dirt took his cue and stepped forward and said, "I am Conway Price. I thank you, my driver thanks you, my wife and children thank you."

Dirt paused for air and emotional discipline. Spider took the slack and said, "What the commander means is to show a portion of our gratitude we are having a party. The Kwajalein VFW has offered us the use of their facility. It is located to the front of your formation. We will stand the tab until the last man leaves or hell freezes over. Dirt and Spider, that's us. On behalf of Double Trouble the best fighter squadron in the Navy."

"In the world," said Dirt.

"In the world," said Spider.

Dirt walked to the first marine in rank and moved swiftly down the line shaking the hand of each marine. It was crowded going in the second and third rank as the Gunny was taken by surprise and had not given the formation the command to open ranks.

Tumble watched the sailors complete their progress through the formation.

"You heard the invitation. We are welcome. We are guests. There will be no fights. Personal property will be respected. The two marines who are female will not harass the male marines."

There was polite laughter from the ranks.

"Gunny, they're yours," said Tumble. "Make sure these marines know how the cow eats the cabbage. Special emphasis on the two women marines. They will be treated with respect. You and two other crew members will personally and safely escort them to quarters. If there are objections, from male or female, then immediately notify me."

"Won't be any objections, sir."

"Good. The marines can enjoy the celebration and a day on the beach tomorrow. Remind the crew we have an afternoon training hop. Dismiss the formation."

"Aye, aye, sir."

Tumble returned the salute, did an about face and walked over to join Bongo, Juan, Rent, and the two Navy fliers.

"You marines talk a lot," said Dirt. "Put on a show. Come on this VFW is a great place."

Tumble smiled and followed. He did not bother explaining to the sailors that Kwaj was a regular Marine stop.

Inside the VFW building was a typical male dominated bar with overtones of Asia, the Pacific, the military, and home. The juke box contained a selection of gold rock and old country. No CDs, 45s only and a source mystery in themselves. A beer was thrust upon Tumble. Quiet would have to wait.

Dirt and Spider rehashed the event as they had seen it. Bongo, the better story teller, represented the Herc. The telling made the event sound like a good time. None would want to repeat it.

"Last time a fighter pilot bought me a beer was in Korea, an OB. Guy had a seven foot tall grandfather clock. He wanted me to fly it back to Japan for him," said Bongo.

"You take it?" asked Spider. ,

"Sure and told him to leave a case of beer with it for the crew."

"Coin of the realm," said Don Juan.

"Docs are educated," said Dirt.

"Yep," Juan said. "Just how are you guys paying for this? You don't come off the boat for a cycle carrying max bucks."

"IOUs."

"IOUs?"

"That's right."

"These fellows know you're sailors?"

"We're naval officers and gentlemen. They know we are good for it."

"In that case, make mine scotch."

Dirt did not blink. He said to the volunteer bartender, "best you got."

"Thanks," said Juan. "Tall glass, no ice, water back."

Juan pulled a five-dollar bill from his pocket and put it on the bar and said, "tip."

The bartender looked at him, smiled wryly and said, "come here often?"

He picked the money off the bar and dropped it in a large glass jar that was labeled for pickled pig feet on one side and the American Cancer Society on the other.

"Don Juan, Don Juan," Tumble said. "Meet CJ. He is post commander and a rocket scientist when not behind the bar. All tips go in the charity jar."

Tumble drank a couple of beers, shelled some peanuts and called it a night. Bongo followed.

Dirt and Spider waved and returned to their host duties.

Chapter Four Tarawa Tourist

Awake at 0600 Tumble knocked on Bongo's door and walked over to the BOQ (bachelor officers quarters) office to bum a cup of coffee from the duty NCO (non commissioned officer). He returned to his room and did twenty minutes of the daily seven exercises.

He knocked on Bongo's door a second time and Bongo came out dressed to run. They started slow and headed toward the beach. The sand trail was lined by sparse grass and tall coconut palms. They turned parallel to the sea and picked up the pace. Approaching the salt water swimming pool they recognized three figures sitting on a concrete picnic table.

"Good morning," said Juan.

Dirt and Spider sat with Juan. They nodded and smiled. A bottle of MacAllan Scotch Whisky filled only with wet shine sat on the table beside them.

"Staying on the beach today, Juan?" said Bongo.

"Thought so. Work on my melanoma research."

"Any word?" Tumble asked the fighter guys.

"Slim. The COD (carrier on board delivery aircraft) will fly in tomorrow. Bring some parts and maintenance people. We'll fly back on as the Bobby Lee sails by."

"Christmas at sea?"

"Navy. We are working our way back to Atsugi for New Years. We'll be in the Sea of Japan the week after that."

"Sea of Japan ops? We'll be there, too."

"Yeah, the North Koreans, the Democratic People's Republic of Korea, the DPRK. They are claiming national waters from Wonsan to the beaches of Honshu. The U.S. Navy is calling bullshit on that. The fleet will operate within that zone. Maintain the right of free passage on the high seas for all. We'll provide combat air patrol sixteen hours a day, 0600 to 2200. You marines will cover the balance of the night with Hornets out of Sakura."

"We'll be flying airborne tanker support for the Marine Hornets and have a ready tanker standing by for the Navy CAP (combat air patrol)."

Christmas week in Australia is summer time and Tumble would not miss the snow. Snow was something to be cleaned off wings and it was cold. He was looking forward to beach time on the Gold Coast. Today would be a training X. Tomorrow would be Brisbane.

The breeze tickled the coconut palm fronds. The temperature was 85 degrees. Tumble took a red and white striped peppermint candy cane from the sunscreen rail above the open swing window. A half dozen of the leave and liberty marines were along for the ride and the rest were experiencing a Kwaj beach day.

Tumble made the takeoff. The sky was clear and the ocean was the aquamarine blue of a girl's eyes he had seen in Bodo, Norway.

Level at ten thousand feet Tumble engaged the Herc auto pilot. He asked Bongo to leave the right seat but stay on the flight deck.

One by one Hostile bought the young marines up from the back. Tumble put them in the right pilot seat, clicked the autopilot off, checked the trim and let each marine fly the Herc. They made gentle turns, climbs, and descents, and speed changes. Tumble kept his hands and feet on the flight controls.

Most marines are good and hard working. The demands made upon the young men and women, by their nation and Corps, are out of proportion to the pay or thanks they receive. Their reward is personal honor and pride. They are loyal to one another and routinely strive against odds to accomplish their assigned duties and missions. Tumble knew whether they served three or thirty years they would remember this flight for the rest of their lives. It would be the time they flew a Marine KC-130 Hercules and it would be a grand, glowing, and daring tale by the time their grandchildren heard it and that was as it should be. Tumble knew the action was not approved but it was easier to get forgiveness than it was to get permission. He knew either nothing would be said or there would be an ass chewing and there never was a good marine who let that threat stop him from doing what he knew to be right.

After each of the marines had their chance to fly and have a smile put on their face Bongo climbed back into the right seat. They still had an official training X to get on a low level flight. Rent gave them a heading for the first point and they turned southeast toward Tarawa.

Tumble pulled the four throttles to flight idle and then bumped them a knob width forward to stay out of the negative torque system range and to silence the gear warning horn and put the red gear handle warning light out. The horn and light were activated when the throttles were pulled to flight idle and the landing gear was not down. He made a coordinated roll to forty-five degrees angle of bank while he momentarily dropped the nose to fifteen degrees low. The Herc speed quickly increased to 250 knots and Tumble brought the nose back to five degrees low and then varied it three to five degrees to maintain 250 knots and a good rate of descent toward the sea.

Tumble glanced at the radar altimeter and cross checked it with the barometric altimeter. He leveled the Herc at five hundred feet above the South Pacific. They would fly lower but five hundred feet was a good altitude to warm up the low level process. The world changes dramatically, for navigating purposes, below five hundred feet.

The blue diamond sparkle of the sea was regularly broken by small islands and many were of the single coconut palm cartoon variety. Other islands were thickly palm forested and they twice saw palm frond thatched huts and islanders who waved to them.

Rent called another turn, checked the timing and had Tumble adjust the speed to 240 knots. A speed that was a multiple of six would allow for easier mental timing calculations over the low level route.

Fifteen minutes later they saw Tarawa. They passed over the island as tourists, as pilgrims. They did not see anyone but there were a few small buildings and what could have been a rough runway. Tarawa was where their Marine Corps predecessors had fought and won a blundering, bloody battle against an Imperial Japanese force. Then, 1943, was a world before zero defects and the marines and their generals had learned quickly. From the mistakes at bloody Tarawa they had gone on to sure but bloody victories throughout the

Pacific. Tarawa is a shrine in the heart of the United States Marine Corps.

"Bourbon?" Asked Juan.

"No. Make it Coca-Cola, double, lots of ice," said Tumble.

They were in the VFW. Tumble was hot and covered with a sticky sweat. Juan and the sailors looked as if they had a start on a good tan and the evening. Targets of opportunity were non-existent. Dirt and Spider were sipping beer. Fighter pilots talk about flying and drinking but ashore the subjects were second to the chase, sex before beer. A Navy chief is second to none at the bar but in the officer corps it was a dark horse. Tumble had never met a flight doc, away from duty, who could not drink and pontificate from sun down to sun up. Juan was into slow bourbon drinking, water back, and pontificating.

"What time do we shove off tomorrow, Tumble?"

"I am on my way to base ops. There should be a message there with our diplomatic clearances. If the times on the dip clearance are as requested we will go at 0630."

"Last call," Bongo said.

"Roger that. How about a run? The breeze is up and the sun is going down."

Juan decided to go with them. The doc had a runners build but it was genetics and not exercise that kept him slim.

It was okay. Tumble wanted a long, slow run to ease out the days tensions, cleanse body and spirit with physical exertion.

Coconut palms outnumbered blades of grass. Interspersed among the palms were various antennas and structures vital to the primary island business of down range missile tracking. Everywhere they ran they saw well used but serviceable bicycles, the preferred mode of island transportation. They stopped to watch a crew of men climbing coconut palms and dropping coconuts to the ground. An idler told them it was to keep the coconuts from falling at an inopportune time and hitting a passerby on the head. A falling coconut could be deadly.

It was dusk and no artificial light was visible beyond the island. The street lights were on but timid. There was no overlap of light and each light stopped abruptly and did not fade gently out into the darkness. They turned their run back toward the Kwaj lodge where they were quartered. Nearby, on a sparse grass area, several Marshall Islanders had gathered into a waiting group.

Tumble recognized a man from the VFW standing near them. He figured he and his friends had zigged and zagged enough to log four miles.

"Let's call it off here," Tumble said.

Tumble approached the VFW acquaintance, a security employee.

"Why are they waiting?" Tumble said.

"Marshallese. We don't let them stay after dark. Most go over to Roi Namur on the boat."

"Why don't they stay here?"

"Too much walks away. A little is worth a lot here."

"Oh?"

"Yeah, it is their island. They protest, of course. They say they should not be isolated; aren't paid enough for their land or labor. Don't like the situation."

"Sounds tough."

"Suppose it is but it is above my pay grade. I do six more months here and then go back to the world."

They were up early for an American breakfast: eggs to order, sausage, potatoes, and toast. It was followed by a big glass of not so cold milk and a cup of very hot coffee.

Tumble had told Rodeo to bag out the fuel. There would be no more over water eco cruise for Mrs. MacFarland's boy.

Tumble looked around the chow hall. It could have been an institutional dining facility anywhere. There was a Christmas tree in one corner and green and gold decorative roping draped about the room as well as green plastic Hong Kong holly with red berries. He made a quick count. All of the marines were present. The excitement was in their eyes and a few had the red look of too much beach. It would not keep them from having a good time with Christmas, and Australia, and Brisbane next.

Chapter Five   Brisbane on Christmas Eve

Australia and the Great Barrier Reef were surreal from 24,000 feet cruise altitude. The flight from Kwajalein took them across the Solomon Islands and the Coral Sea. It lasted five cups of sequentially harsher tasting coffee and was uneventful.

Bongo was in the left seat and swished the landing on the 10,000 plus feet runway at YBBN, Brisbane International Airport. The Herc was dwarfed by the Quantas Airbus A-380, the world's largest passenger jet, in the next parking spot. It was a great photo op with the red kangaroo logo Quantas jet in the background.

Gunny Simpson had the marines in formation. They took more photos.

"Have a good time. Don't be stupid. Any town can be a tough town. Keep a buddy," Tumble said.

He turned to Rodeo and said, "Put them in a school circle. Use your best NCO motivational technique. Make sure they understand the rules, written and unwritten. If we screw this up no one will have this opportunity again."

A chartered bus took them to the hotel. The hotel was in walking distance of downtown Brisbane.

South of the equator, below the Tropic of Capricorn, Christmas is a summer celebration and a fine one. Brisbane is a bustling town and located near Australia's Gold Coast. Good choices for Christmas leave.

"Take a look at this," Bongo said. He was standing at the third floor window of Tumble's hotel room. They had spent Christmas Eve day sightseeing. Now, at dusk, they looked down and saw the crowded street. It had been so all day but now the flavor was changing.

They could see women dressed festively, heels and pearls, spaghetti strap dresses, short skirts, styled hair. Bongo opened the window. The voices from below carried a good natured and excited tone.

The temperature was pleasant. The throng had crowded the cars from the street. The air was clean and clear. Music spilled from restaurants and bars as the doors and windows were opened. Sounds melded, separated, flowed in strata and formed a mood enhancing backdrop that stirred excitement in time to the blood pulsing through their veins.

"Absolutely great, this is going to be absolutely great," said Bongo."It is a once in a lifetime night. They will call us liars when we get back to the Rock."

Stepping out of the hotel door Tumble, Bongo, and Don Juan were immediately engulfed in the crowd. The tangible tingle of femininity was everywhere carried by sight, sound, and scent. There was a low current of male voices and shouts and upon that current rode the tinkling soprano notes of female laughter. The women wore perfume and the scents were sharp, or musk, or floral and formed a pleasant and layered olfactory mist.

"Tumble, we have traditions to uphold. We are aviators on liberty in paradise. You look like you lost your puppy. Look around. Soak it up. This is as good as it gets," said Bongo.

"No one will ever believe us," Tumble said. He laughed. He knew Bongo was right. He could smell his recent separation as if it were a week dead albatross hanging around his neck.

"I'm not planning on writing a book. Nobody believes anything said at happy hour. Hear a good story, wait two weeks and make it yours," said Bongo.

First beer is on me," said Tumble.

"I thought you would never come through. Make mine scotch," said Juan. He knew bourbon would be hard to find.

"First bar this side of the street," said Bongo.

Tumble saw a couple coming directly toward himself and his two friends. He stepped left to allow them to pass between himself and Bongo. The girl was medium height and her left arm encircled the waist of an Aussie big enough to play pro rugby.

The girl was made for admiration. Her blonde hair was cut shoulder length. She was wearing a shimmering, wine red dress, top cut low and hem high, mid thigh. The dress had thread like shoulder straps for insurance. Her shoes had heels the clarity of cut crystal and the street light through them radiated a rainbow prism. Her figure was last seen on a Vargas calendar.

Three feet from Tumble the woman gave a high pitched short laugh. Her left arm tensed, squeezed her bosom against the big Aussie and swelled her breasts in the low cut dress until the pink-brown aureoles peeked out.

"Yanks," she said. "Yanks are in Brisbane on Christmas Eve." The way she said Brisbane reduced it to a one syllable word.

She dropped her arm from the Aussie. She extended her right hand holding a wine glass, extended her index finger until it touched Tumble's chest.

"Merry Christmas," she said in her wine voice.

Merry Christmas," Tumble said with a smile.

She threw both arms around Tumble's neck and her right arm gimbaled like a precision instrument. She did not spill a drop of the red wine. She pressed her breasts firmly against his chest.

Languorously, she brought her right ankle around Tumble's left calf, wrapped and moved her leg up to the back of his knee showing an appreciative audience finely defined calf and thigh musculature and a strip of champagne lace across the hip. She thrust her pelvis hard against him and deeply kissed him.

Overpowered by the hormonal rush Tumble was momentarily paralyzed. He felt his involuntary response, the heat of the woman's body, and the probing rush of her tongue. Then, she was cool, smooth. She gently rolled the tip of her tongue across each of his eyelids and the scent of red wine lay like velvet on her tongue. He could feel the cool breeze across his eye lids afterwards. He inhaled her heated fragrance, soft with sea and roses. He felt her release him, his eyes began to focus. She stepped back and he could see her full length.

The woman stood with a curious and amused look on her face, left arm akimbo. The blue bed room eyes disappeared in a laugh. She made a half step forward and gave him a sisterly kiss on the cheek.

"Merry Christmas; a Brisbane memory for you," she said. Her voice was conversational.

The big Aussie gave a pleasant laugh and his eyes showed neither anger nor distrust.

"Sorry about you other two," the big man said. He shook hands with Bongo and Don Juan. "She kisses yanks on the street. Don't do it myself.

This is the best night of the year in Brisbane. You will enjoy it."

Arm in arm the couple walked on past, put their heads together and laughed at their little joke. Tumble, Bongo, and Juan turned as one to watch her go.

She had walked a half dozen steps when she stopped, turned her head back, and saw them watching. She smiled.

"Glad we could make them happy," said Juan.

"What a great country," said Bongo.

"Wonder if they could use another doctor down here?" said Juan. "I can be out of the Navy in a year."

Tumble stood silent, mesmerized. Juan clapped his hands beneath Tumble's nose. Tumble focused his eyes on Juan as his mind caught up with the present.

"I don't get it," said Bongo. "I am better looking than you, a lot better looking. I cannot believe she did not pick me out of this bunch."

"She thought Tumble looked safe," Juan said.

"Luck counts two points just like skill. I was going to buy the first beer, but not now, you owe me homage," said Tumble.

They made token stops in noisy bars and did not finish their beers in a couple. The ever changing street was a more enjoyable place to spend time. Tumble was the first to run up a white flag.

"Let's take a break, somewhere quieter, a piano bar maybe."

Juan nodded, made a fist with a thumb extended to the building beside them. A street level sign with an arrow pointing to a step-down staircase was to his immediate left. The red neon sign proclaimed a wine bar and a neon yellow light sketched a grand piano.

"Don't tell me you did not see that," said Juan.

The handrail and steps were black wrought iron. The steps were crosshatched and open like a heavy chain link fence. The solid handrail was covered with layer upon layer of black, chipped paint. The steps led below street level to a concrete landing. The landing was swept clean but it had the trapped scent of stale cigarette smoke. The door was thick wood and inset in the top half was an opaque and dimpled glass window with heavy, imbedded wire. The bar logo and stylized piano were repeated in colored paints on the opaque glass. Muted voices and the sound of a single piano came from behind the door.

Bongo pushed and then pulled to open the door. He gave a shrug and a grin. Past the threshold the wall was paneled with a medium tone wood of unrecognized grain. Good, local watercolors were on the walls and discrete prices were posted in the lower right corners. The wrought iron steps began again and led down two more steps to a waffle design wrought iron landing from which the bar proper could be surveyed.

The light level was artificial dusk. Gilt frame mirrors and paintings were positioned about the walls. There was enough vegetation around the floor to provide cover for several large and previously unknown marsupials. There were booths against the walls and the seats were upholstered in dark red leather and the tables were a dark, polished, tropical wood.

The background music came from a vintage grand piano located off room center and at the near end of the long bar. The crowd was festive though subdued in comparison to the one on the street.

The ladies were dressed for the cocktail hour and a few of the men wore jackets, no ties. The air conditioning made a valiant effort to cool the packed room.

Tumble noticed a few beers in heavy, pint glasses among the wine glasses. He decided to skip the wine. He had had too much beer to make a switch. Tumble felt a nudge from Bongo.

"What?" Tumble said. He saw Bongo and Juan looking toward a booth. There, sat three women and a man.

"They are with someone," said Tumble.

"They are always with someone," said Bongo.

"I'm just here for the beer," said Tumble.

"I'm here for both," said Juan.

Tumble felt himself smile before he knew why. A young woman in the booth, pretty in any land, was looking into his eyes. Her complexion was dark olive and her hair gloss black curls matching the color and sparkle of her eyes which were framed by dark, fashionable glasses.

"Let's go for it," said Bongo.

"Two is in hot," said Juan.

Tumble hesitated. He felt himself take a step back against the wrought iron landing.

"Don't be in such a hurry to go, yank. We are friendly," said a feminine Australian accented voice. It held neither a force of command or desire but rang of potential.

Tumble stopped and that was a decision in itself. He felt Juan's hand on his elbow.

"Sit and talk, sit and talk, partner. The drinks are on Bongo," said Juan.

Tumble looked at the girl. She was talking to the other girls in the booth. The wine drinking man was gone.

"Never cut the herd early. It spooks them," said Bongo.

"They are people," said Tumble.

"We are here for a week," said Bongo.

Juan was three steps ahead of them.

"Damn sailors are slippery," said Bongo and he propelled Tumble ahead with a push in the back.

The booth seats had three-quarter backs. They were high enough for token privacy and low enough to allow the occupants to see over and be seen.

Juan slid in on one side of the leather upholstered, horse shoe seat and Bongo on the other. The arrangement left the three women between two men. Tumble stood for a moment before Bongo noticed him. He moved closer to the girl on his left and made room for Tumble. Bongo was into his act.

"Awkward," said the brunette with the glasses.

"You know the problem with fishing?" Bongo said. "When you catch them you have to keep them or throw them back."

There was polite group laughter.

"You never know what you will have to keep, clean, and eat," said the woman next to Bongo. She gave him an unblinking look.

"So, names or no names? You have names and we have names. Mine is Bongo, that's Don Juan and the silent man is Tumble.

"What odd names," said the dark haired woman.

"They are yanks and therefore they are odd," said the woman next to Bongo.

"Actually, I cannot believe those are real names," said the dark haired girl next to Juan.

"Real enough," said Juan.

"Okay, names good enough for Christmas Eve. The new rule is no last names tonight," said the dark haired girl. She turned to Juan, tapped his forearm, and moved her lips close to his ear and sotto voce said, "Trade places with me."

"Right," said Juan.

Juan squeezed by and concentrated on the short blonde. He saw no reason to spend time on the dark haired, dusky beauty. She seemed attracted to Tumble.

There was laughter. The temptress of the gentle taunt smiled. Her lips were dark red and a small white sliver shown between her lips. She had a tiny diamond stud on the left side of her nose. Slowly, enjoying his discomfort, she reached across the table and drew her crossed hands across the back of Tumble's hand. Her fingers left a trail of heat. He could feel the individual hairs on the back of his hand as she withdrew her touch.

"Pick some names," said Bongo.

"I'm Baile," said the girl beside Bongo.

"I'm Madonna," the blonde said. "Yes, it is my real name."

"What name do you want me to use?" said the dark haired woman.

"Abeer, you are reading too many Gothic romances. Her name is Abeer, and it means fragrant or something like that. Now, we are friends. Tell us how you come to be in Brisbane on Christmas Eve," said Baile.

Bongo took the lead and told the story. Juan provided humorous commentary. Tumble minded his manners and drank Bongo's beer.

After a lively half hour the girls, lemming like, arose and moved off as one to the ladies room.

"Note comparison time," said Bongo.

"I might be in love. No, I am in love. My mama always wanted me to marry a nice Catholic girl," said Juan.

"Yeah, and her mama wants her to marry a doctor," said Tumble.

"Everyone will be happy, then," said Bongo. "Tumble, if you are not careful you will discourage Abeer."

Tumble ignored him. He signaled the waitress.

The ladies returned. They went into the street where the crowd swelled, moved, and counter moved. There was no clear flow direction but individual progress could be made in any direction. It was a de facto pedestrian only street. The feminine voices of the crowd rode, like oil on water, the crest of masculine shouts and they smoothed the edges of the evening sounds.

The police were present but tolerant. They looked for dangerous acts or gross violations of decorum or property. The police moved through the crowd garnering their fair share of volunteer kisses. Tumble saw more than one pretty young lady grab a handful of police rump for a friendly squeeze. No girl was arrested for assault on a police officer.

"I do not bite, not now at least," Abeer said.

"No, uh, ah..."

"You don't like me?"

"I like you just fine. Beautiful, lively, conversant."

"Available."

"Available?"

"I said that to shock you, perhaps. I am looking for a nice Christmas holiday, however."

"I was looking for a restful one."

"Oh good, it is a test. I enjoy a good test. I have often taken a first. It is Christmas. We will visit a bit. You don't have to accept gifts just because they are offered."

Tumble stopped. Abeer stopped. He faced her. It was a mistake in resolve. He knew so when he looked at her. In the street lights he saw a delightful smile, a glint of white teeth, and startling black eyes past the subtle, dark tartan, colored rims of her glasses. She wore a black silk, sheath dress, simple and modestly cut. She held his eyes with hers. He placed his right hand lightly behind her neck and smiled. The kiss came. The light touch was sharp and immediate like bourbon on cracked ice, cool to the lip and warm on the tongue. Heat traveled the length of his body and was followed by a delightful ripple of coolness. His mind was consumed by the intensity of the moment.

"What now, yank?"

"I am at my limit."

"Okay, we will have a good time. You will remember this Christmas the rest of your life."

"I am sure you are right. Let's have a beer."

"Yes, I do believe I would like one."

They walked the street like old friends, perhaps lovers once, but still comfortable with one another. A quarter of an hour later they found the others.

Bongo had acquired a didigeridoo, a wooden aboriginal wind instrument sold in a tourist version.

He was sounding low notes on it while Juan shook a rain stick.

"Tourist," said Baile.

"We have to attend midnight mass at St. Patrick's. Please come with us," said Madonna.

"Sure," said Bongo.

Juan shrugged a yes.

"You attend mass?" Bongo said to Abeer.

"Sure, my grandparents are from Goa."

"Goa?"

"World history, 16th century, Portuguese, Jesuit missionaries, India, Goa," said Abeer.

"Guess I will have to look that up," said Tumble. "No thanks, though. I'm RTB."

"RTB?"

"Return to base, going back to the hotel."

"Good night," said Abeer.

Juan and Bongo were laughing as he walked away. Madonna and Baile looked at Abeer.

In the hotel room Tumble took the two, 50 ml bottles of JW Red from the mini bar. He called the front desk and told them to bring two more.

He pulled the window curtain back and sat, in the dark, facing the window. He watched the street party fade. He sipped the scotch leavened with cool tap water.

They came as he knew they would. His small son, gone forever, was smiling. His wife, gone too in a different way, was beautiful even in her anguish, tears, and anger. He slept in the chair.

Christmas Eve in Brisbane was a mid summers night revel. Christmas Day was different and that difference woke Tumble. The street was ghostly silent.

Tumble ached. He took three aspirin, put his running clothes on and did fifteen minutes of pushups and sit ups. It was 7 a.m. local.

He started slow and continued slow for forty-five minutes and finished slow. The air was filled with the summer scents of flowers and cut grass and he saw bees buzzing about a city park. There was a hint of the underlying city redolence of old concrete with trapped odors of city life. The litter from the previous night was minimal. A yellow dog, with heavy nursing teats, ignored him as it sniffed about. He finished his run back at the hotel.

"Good morning," Tumble said to the hotel desk clerk. "Where is everyone?"

"Home or the Gold Coast, the beach. It is Christmas Day." The desk clerk, a slim fiftyish, balding man gave a friendly smile and a shoulder shrug. He was resigned to his duty.

"It is beach weather isn't it? Any place nearby open for breakfast?"

"That will be hard to find. There is some coffee ready in the back. Habit I picked up from two years in Seattle, Starbucks and Peet's."

Tumble was sweating freely and breathing easy. He felt better than he had a right to feel. The aspirin and the run had done their job. A cup of coffee would be the topper. He helped himself, wished the clerk a Merry Christmas and turned to walk to his room.

"I have a note for a marine. Who are you?"

"MacFarland."

"Right, this is for you. Your mates will be by and pick you up for a beach trip."

The clerk handed a folded note to Tumble. He did not seem to think it amiss he could tell the marine the contents of the folded note.

"Thanks."

The clerk picked up a magazine and settled back with a cup of coffee for a slow day.

Back in the room Tumble finished his coffee. He wanted a second cup. He turned the water faucet full hot in the bathroom sink. The temperature reached a scalding level, just what he wanted. He searched his bag and found his backup packets of instant coffee. It would be better than no coffee. He emptied a finger size packet of instant coffee into his cup and ran hot water over it. He put it beside the sink, stripped and started the shower.

There was a knock at the door. It was most likely the maid or Bongo. He wrapped himself with a bath towel and opened the door just wide enough to check. There, stood Abeer. She smiled.

Tumble was off guard and he paused.

"Let me in," she said.

"I'm showering."

"That's fine," she said pushing gently past him. "I will wait. I am here to take you to the beach. The others are there."

Tumble picked up his coffee and turned back to Abeer. Perspiration from the run was still flowing down his torso.

"Oh, coffee," she said. "Mind if I have a bit?"

Abeer lifted the cup from his fingers with her right hand. She ran her left index finger down his chest leaving a small wake of pleasure. She stopped at his navel, looked at her finger; saw it damp with perspiration. She laughed.

"Take that shower," she said.

Tumble grabbed a change of clothes and walked into the bath. He completed a long shower and dressed in the bath. He came out in shorts and a tee shirt.

"You think you needed to dress in there?" Abeer said.

Tumble ignored the comment. He was not sure how to answer. He was not ready to offer or receive encouragement. He sensed it would take but little for either of them.

"What's the scoop?"

"Scoop? I am to pick you up and take you to our caravan at the beach. Bring your swim things."

Abeer drove. It took Tumble a few miles to accustom himself to traveling on the left side of the road. The novelty of the driving gone Tumble watched Abeer. Her nearness and femininity were almost overpowering to his senses, there, within the confines of the car. The street kiss Christmas Eve had been sport. They were not touching yet he was aware of her body heat, a palpable pathway. No conscious decision is a decision. Like a still hunter Tumble waited to see what would come down the path.

They talked about the countryside and Christmas in summer. They drove past campsites by the hundred. Tents and trailers were near the beach approaches or on the beach. Families moved about cooking, swimming, or sitting in canvas manufactured shade.

The fabled Gold Coast is south of Brisbane and stretches for miles and is bounded by the South Pacific. Tumble, being a well trained marine, immediately noticed many women sun bathers were topless. The practitioners ran the age gamut. Many, when they stood, would fasten their swim suit top or slip on a tee shirt before walking about or swimming. Others strolled about or swam unconstrained.

Abeer took Tumble's hand and led him among the tents and people. There, under a blue and white awning, they found their friends. All were dressed for the beach and lounging with cool, condensation beaded drinks near at hand. Christmas carols came from the radio.

"You are just in time for lunch, partner," said Bongo.

Juan, wearing blue running shorts for a swimsuit, stirred himself from a beach chair without a word. There was a self satisfied air about him. He moved to a charcoal grill to check the coals.

Madonna stood at his shoulder, a Coke in her left hand and the exposed swell of her breasts pressed familiarly against the back of his shoulder. She placed her right hand finger tips at the small of Juan's back and drew them, like feathers, to the nape of his neck. She stopped there, leaned forward and flicked a darting tongue into his ear. Juan's back muscles visibly quivered.

"Soda or beer?" said Abeer.

Tumble accepted a soda. He looked about and saw a small Christmas tree on one end of a folding table and decorative tinsel ropes of gold, silver, green, and red twined about rigid tent poles.

Abeer left him and went into the tent. She emerged in a slash of saffron orange bikini. The color contrasted, complemented, and emphasized her dusky skin. Her figure was generous yet taunt.

"How about a smear of lotion?" She said to Tumble.

"What?" Tumble said. His hearing had not caught up with his seeing.

"She speaks English. She wants you to put sun lotion on her back," Baile said.

They laughed.

Tumble took the proffered lotion bottle. Abeer turned her back to him and pulled the bow at the back of her bikini top. It came loose and she held it somewhat in place, more exposed than covered.

Tumble sat his soda on the table, put lotion on his hands and touched her exposed back. Abeer gave a small yelp, jumped, and turned to face him. She playfully slapped at his chest with her bikini top. She faced him, hands on hip.

"Warm those hands first. Rub them together. You have been holding an ice cold can. It was like being slathered with an ice cube."

She looked straight into his eyes, smiled broadly, almost laughing. She crossed her arms over her breasts, bikini top dangling from her left hand and turned her back to him.

"Do it right," she said.

The others laughed but did not take particular note of the incident. Tumble was appreciative.

They ate good Australian beef and shrimp and an exotic fruit salad. They drank good wine from Western Australia. Afterwards, the others went to walk or swim. Abeer held Tumble back and offered to make coffee.

"I know about your difficulty," she said while putting a small, propane stove on the table. "I am sorry, and as much as I can, I understand.

Tumble picked up a Swan Beer someone had brought in from Perth. He looked at her. He drank deeply. He did not comment.

"Don't believe me? That is an egocentric position. In it you make the assumption you are the only person with the capability to hear or punish or understand. You demean the ability of others to empathize, to help. It is rude at the very best."

What she said was not dissimilar to what his wife had said when they had parted. Perhaps it was true but that was a long way from acceptance. His son, whom he could no longer accurately picture and he refused to look at a photo, was dead. He was a contributor to that death. He owed suffering and self chastisement as punishment for himself.

Abeer brushed lightly against him. It was bare thigh against bare thigh. Shock waves coursed through his being. He put guilt aside. He accepted the idea of what he knew would come.

She sensed his moment of decision and faced him. Her breasts, minimally contained, were against his chest. He felt the coolness, and smoothness, and firmness of the rounded curve of her stomach against his. It was the slightest of intimate touching and he tasted the moist perfume of her breath. He did not want a way out. He took her hands in his, gently moved them to the small of her back and kissed her.

Her lips were smooth, cool, and just past them teeth barely parted, and heated tongue. Her body pressed against his and they were conscious of each point of contact.

Chapter Six New Years Eve at the Carp Pond

Affection and sadness ruled the emotions when the marines left Australia. There was a small crowd. No one departed without someone to see them off. Gunny Simpson's double count and roll call showed all marines present. Tumble counted the correct number of marines and considered it to be a minor miracle.

Abeer saw Tumble off with a kiss and a playful pat on the rump. It gave the assembled marines a laugh.

"Come back when you can," Abeer said.

"Sure," Tumble said.

They both knew the finish line had been in sight from the start. The intensity of the relationship had been sustainable for a week. The memories would be all there were but they were perfect memories.

Juan and Madonna were a different story. Their affection was deep and past the moment. Their good-byes were painful and sad to see. Madonna had tears in her eyes when Juan was the last to board the engines running Hercules. Coming through the crew entrance door he turned right to sit with the passengers vice coming up to the flight deck as he usually did.

Bongo could have stayed longer but he had no problem leaving. Back on the Rock, for New Years Eve, there would be something to do.

The non-stop return flight was uneventful and long. The 3,600 gallon, internal, fuselage fuel tank unique to the KC-130 tanker gave them the range and allowed for a landing with fuel to spare. They stopped at Okinawa. They could not make the flight on to Sakura before field closing time. The marines, not from the Rock, would stay in transient barracks for the New Year. It was a small price to pay for Christmas week in Australia. The airfield was closed New Years Day. The flight on to Sakura would be on 2 January.

They cleared customs at base operations and saw the marines bused away and then taxied the Herc down to the squadron flight line. Juan said he was going to quarters and sleep. Tumble and Bongo walked up to the quarterdeck area topside of the hangar. The duty officer, First Lieutenant Leif Erikson, aka Viking, was there as was Sailor Mann the squadron operations officer, a major and third in the squadron chain of command after the commanding officer and executive officer.

"Happy New year," said Sailor.

"You too. Surprised to see you here. Thought you would be at the Air Force O Club for the big party," said Tumble

"I will be. There is more flying for you and your crew so there are more orders to cut and enough flying to go around. We're sending three ships to the Philippines, two more to Korea, one to Hawaii, two hangar queens, one at Singapore rework, and you go to Sakura. Lots of people not yet back from Christmas leave; everybody here flies."

"Fine by me, what is the scoop?"

"We'll all meet up in Sakura in a week. You will be there for two. The first week is tanker refueling qualifications for the Hornet pilots, day and night quals. The second week you'll be joined by more Hercs. The CO and I will be there. The XO will hold the fort down here."

"Sea of Japan ops?"

"Yes. The Navy will operate in international waters inside the Sea of Japan, the East Sea as the Koreas prefer to call it, but outside the 12 nautical mile limit. The Navy will exercise free passage on the high seas and emphasize the right of all nations to such passage.

Not being stupid, however, they will keep combat air patrols over the fleet 24 hours a day. The carrier CAP will operate 16 hours a day. The Navy will take 0600 to 2200 and the fighters out of Sakura will cover the fleet the other 8 hours. That will give the Navy a maintenance break."

Tumble was familiar with the scenario. It was practiced worldwide where ever there was an infringement or challenge to the right of free passage. In the upcoming operation the tanker Herc would provide in flight refueling to the shore based Marine Corps fighter aircraft. The aerial refueling reduced the number of fighter cycles and increased the time on station as the Marine fighters covered the balance of night.

The KC-130 Hercules tanker would maintain an airborne station out of the way but near the CAP area and provide jet fuel as needed. In addition to the airborne tanker there would be a second tanker manned on a hot pad ready for a short notice launch and a cold but ready tanker backing that one. The other tankers would be spares to take up the slack for broken aircraft or the need to increase the number of on station tankers. No fighter would go short of fuel.

The aerial tanking qualification is a perishable commodity for the fighter pilot. The requalification would start with day plugs and advance to night plugs. The tanker crew would spend hours each day and night drilling sky holes as the receiver aircraft cycled up, each with a new pilot, for their appropriate requalification.

"This is great, Bongo. It's what I signed up for," Tumble said as they made their way down the ladder well.

"Sure is. I figured we would be on the ground for a couple of weeks as punishment for receiving a good deal. I do have a lot of admin work to catch up."

"Don't kid yourself. You would just interfere with Staff Sergeant Johnson and his marines. No telling how many extra hours they spend unscrewing stuff after you have helped them."

"Okay. I won't interfere with Johnson's good job done. Guess I'll spend New Year's Day doing laundry."

"I'll catch Rodeo. The boys will be finishing the post flight and we need to make sure they know the schedule. Tomorrow off and check with the duty NCO for launch time the day after."

"Okay. I'll load our bags in the Blue Bird while you do that. We can hit the club for a couple of beers."

They took the habu trail short cut around the backside of the runway. The trail was dirt and gravel and both sides of the car were brushed by elephant grass that was the home to a quick, deadly, local pit viper called the habu and also the name adopted for the Air Force's formerly Okinawa based SR-71 high altitude and extremely fast reconnaissance jet.

The lights were on at the Officers Club and the parking lot was deserted. Tumble checked his watch, 2045, early. They walked in. The club was quiet as if closed but left unlocked. Tumble and Bongo were the only customers.

The bartender, a moon lighting sailor, pretended to be busy. Finally, he sighed audibly, looked at his watch, and arched his eyebrows as an offer of service.

"Two beers," said Bongo. He was determined to stay in a good mood. He had been to Brisbane and the sailor had not.

"Cold beers," said Tumble. He gave his nice guy, big tipper smile.

The bartended served the beers; no offer of a glass. He said: "The action is over at the Air Force base. All the big New Years Eve parties are at the clubs there. We are closing here and this is last call."

"Last call," said Tumble. He looked at the bartender who did not smile.

"That's what I said."

The bartender turned his back to them and began to stack glasses. In the mirror behind the bar they could see him mouth the word, "duh."

"We'll take a case, partner," said Bongo.

The bartender slowly turned, made a show of tightening his face muscles and pursing his lips. He locked his elbows straight and placed his hands on the bar. He smirked, drawing it out, savoring the moment, his victory.

"Partner," he said twisting the word. "Partner, everything that crosses this bar crosses it open."

Bongo locked eyes with the bartender. He reached into the small, zippered pocket on the left, upper sleeve of his flight suit. He pulled out a can of snuff and two twenty dollar bills. He opened the snuff and took a small pinch. He looked directly into the bartender's eyes. He returned the snuff can to the pocket and put the two twenties on the bar.

"Open them, partner, twenty-four."

"The bartender hesitated, thought better, then brought up a handful of beers and began to open them.

"Box 'em," said Bongo.

"I am going to tell the O Club manager about this," said the bartender. He pushed the case of open beers across the bar.

Bongo remained silent until the change was presented. He stuffed a single dollar bill into the tip jar.

"You do what you think is best," Bongo said.

Tumble looked at the bartender and slowly shook his head.

As they walked away they heard the bartender mumble, "assholes." It was just loud enough to sop his attitude and low enough to claim a misunderstood word.

Tumble and Bongo had already moved past the moment.

Even semi-tropical islands can get chilly. Okinawa is 26 degrees north of the equator and has the occasional winter weather day. New Years Eve was one of them. It was cold and a light mist was falling on the island. The water beaded on their leather flight jackets.

"I don't want to go to the Air Farce club tonight," said Tumble.

"I don't either. Let's drink the beer," said Bongo.

Outside the Officers Club was an ornamental carp pond. A Navy nurse had once told him they were koi. Tumble wasn't sure of the difference between gold fish and carp and koi but knew this was called a carp pond. The white and gold and orange fish were swimming about and they did not know their names. The pond was shielded from street view by heavy, semi-tropical vegetation and on the club side was a grassed area and a half dozen palm trees. It gave the carp pond a modicum of privacy.

"How about here?" Tumble said. He took a beer from the case Bongo was carrying and sat on the damp grass, back against a palm.

Bongo placed the beer between them and sat cross legged on the grass. They could hear the hum of the pump that circulated water which fell and gurgled over artificial rocks. They watched the bartender and night O Club manager leave. They were not noticed. They were silent through three beers

"Have a good time?" said Bongo.

They could see over the plants on the street side of the carp pond, past the high rise BOQs, all the way to the 9,000 feet runway and across that the aircraft hangars. All was in silhouette from sharply defined to blurry as if modeled from cotton balls and spray painted in shades of gray and black. Behind them they could see the glow of lights from the town just outside the gate. The streets were crowded with traffic and the sounds of excitement stabbed in their direction and reached them as backdrop.

"Yeah, yeah, I had a good time."

"Thought so."

"I'm coming down now."

"Get over it. Get on with life. It can't be all Marine Corps all the time."

They drank the beers and put the empty bottles in the box and the box in the trunk of the Blue Bird. They left the car in the parking lot and walked to the BOQ.

Tumble was asleep when the New Year arrived.

Chapter Seven Pheasant Hunters

The Monday morning flight was smooth. Several Hornet pilots completed their day tanker qualification. The Herc would fly another day hop in the afternoon. Tuesday the Herc crew would fly day hops and a night hop and they would fly whatever it took for four days after that until the two squadrons of Hornet pilots had refreshed their qualifications. Saturday would be a cleanup day if any quals were left or a no fly day for catch up maintenance.

Tumble was in base operations getting a weather briefing from the staff sergeant weather guesser when the corporal from flight filing signaled for his attention and directed him to a phone. The caller was Sailor Mann.

"Tumble, how is it going there?"

"Good so far. Frontal system headed this way by the weekend. It could interfere with the quals."

"Saw that. The front should be clearing as the fleet comes into position. I have an add-on flight for you."

"Oh, we already have something every day."

"The CO wants you to run to Cheju-do this afternoon for a drop. The return pickup will be Friday. The C-12 was scheduled to make the flight, morale run, but it is hard down, parts on order. You will be taking pheasant hunters. The Army has a rest and recreation hunting facility there."

"I've heard of it. Who am I taking?"

"Our Group XO is there to go along with the fighter group CO plus six others. There is a horse holder, Lieutenant Colonel Ludlow. He'll be your point of contact."

"Okay, we don't have time to run them over before the next flight. Tell the bottle cap colonel to have his group ready at 1730. We'll gas and go after the quals. It will be a long day for us."

"It's why they pay you. When do you fly tomorrow?"

"Afternoon, 1400. It will give us time for day quals and we'll roll into the night work. Early dark, you know. By the way, Friday is make-up day. We're looking at three hops, two days to get the wing and group staff guys qualified and a long night period to finish them up. It'll be a backup, too, in case there are maintenance problems or someone needs a few extra plugs. The fighters want the weekend for maintenance so they will be ready for the start of ops. It makes a Friday Cheju pickup too hard so how about Saturday?'

"Nope, in fact you will have to fly Saturday to qual the Group CO so he can fly Sea of Japan ops on Monday. The hunters will have to cut their pheasant hunt short by a day. You can pick them up mid morning on Thursday, maybe early afternoon and still make your Friday schedule. Maybe need a short slide. It will be a long day."

"So will Friday."

"Tell your congressman or your mother. They might care. I don't."

"Roger that. You coming up?"

"Wouldn't miss it. See you Sunday."

Tumble gave the crew the news. They accepted it with a shrug and routine whining. Never count on off time in the Marines.

The afternoon training flight went as advertised. After landing they taxied to base operations and called for a fuel truck. Tumble and Rent went inside to check the weather and file an ICAO flight plan to Cheju-do and back. Tumble sent Bongo over to hold hands with the passengers.

The horse holder, the fighter group CO and Tumble's group XO, from the Rock, would arrive at their pleasure, not the schedule. They had to pee on the grass and mark their territory. Marine transport plane commanders did not set schedules for colonels. The other passengers were waiting in the passenger area. Bongo had Hostile take them to the plane.

A staff car, CO's flag attached, drove onto the flight line and up to the Herc. The colonels got out, returned salutes and entered the Herc. Lieutenant Colonel Ludlow, tail wagging, pulled Tumble aside.

"Captain, I hear there is a problem with a Friday afternoon pickup?"

"Yes sir, we have a tight training schedule Friday. There is no way to work in a flight to Cheju-do. We will pick you up mid-morning Thursday, maybe a 1300 pickup at latest. We'll have to work it out with the fighters. You may have to ride through a tanking qual on the return trip," Tumble said. He noticed Ludlow was a slick pocket, no aviator wings.

Lieutenant Colonel Ludlow smiled with his lips. The corners of his eyes did not wrinkle.

"The hunt goes through Friday, Captain," said Ludlow.

"Yes sir, I cannot do a Friday pickup and fly the required qualification flights for the Hornets. I will arrive at Cheju-do at 1300 Thursday to pick up your party unless you want to wait until Saturday."

"Saturday is out, Captain. You will be flying Saturday to qualify the group commanding officer."

Tumble noticed the use of the full title vice the usual "C.O.". The horse holder was emphasizing the importance of the individual being discussed. Tumble wondered how much the Group CO actually knew and how much the bottle cap colonel was not telling him. Ludlow wanted the hunt to go as he had advertised it. He had set it up from the start and was on a ground exchange tour with the air wing and this was his chance to look good. The Sea of Japan ops were relatively short notice, Washington making a point. Still, Tumble was surprised the CO had not cancelled his personal plans.

"Yes sir, we will pick you up Thursday," Tumble said.

Lieutenant Colonel Ludlow stared at Tumble. He did not speak. It was an old intimidation trick. Tumble had seen it used many times. However, he was flying a Herc and not a time machine. There was no way to accommodate the preferred, pheasant hunter schedule and complete the assigned mission.

It was a clear, cold, crisp day. They flew west over the lake within a lake near Fukuoka. The airport at Cheju-do has a 9,800 feet precision instrument approach main runway and a perpendicular, 6,600 feet non-instrument runway. The instrument runway is parallel to the sea and the shorter runway starts at the sea and runs toward rising terrain southeast of the airport. Along the way the earth rises steeply from sea level to a 6,400 feet mountain peak.

Transportation was waiting for the pheasant hunters. They exited with their gear and waved friendly good-byes to the crew.

"See you Thursday, sir, 1300," Tumble said to Lieutenant Colonel Ludlow.

"Right, Captain."

Lieutenant Colonel Ludlow knew Tumble's name. He chose not to use it. He preferred the more formal and impersonal way in addressing Tumble. The fighter group CO and Tumble's group XO did not speak to him. A bad sign as it was normal for the VIP passenger to glad hand the aircraft commander and say thanks.

They were uncovered, hatless, on the flight line. It was a FOD or foreign object damage precaution and practiced by marines after more than one jet engine had been damaged by sucking in a marine's head cover. Tumble was grateful for the small favor. The Marine Corps, a naval service, did not salute uncovered. Tumble had rarely begrudged giving a salute but he did not like or trust Lieutenant Colonel Ludlow as he seemed to be the kind of officer promoted on the golf course or by pimping pheasant hunts for the boss.

Two busy and uneventful days followed. Hornet pilots cycled up to plug time after time, pushing refueling probes into blossomed drogues trailing eighty feet behind each wing of the KC-130. The fighter pilots worked hard renewing and honing their skills at twenty thousand feet and 250 knots. Day and night they worked practicing with radioed instructions and then, radio silence, using light signals from the tanker.

Thursday morning there was light snow. The wind kicked up and began regularly gusting to thirty-five knots and often more. The air station did not have a cross wind runway. When the wind shifted around ninety degrees to the runway it gusted beyond the published safe operating limits of the Hercules aircraft. Currently the wind was forty-five degrees to the runway but that could change.

Tumble studied the forecast. The wind was currently in limits. The weather might force the cancellation of the afternoon training flights. There was no way to tell. Now was the best of a bad time period to make the Cheju-do pickup.

Sergeant Hostile Lopez passed a cup of black coffee to Tumble. Hostile was the radio operator and load master. The newer J model Herc would not have the R.O. designated crewmember but the loadmaster would be kept. In the meanwhile the crews liked the legacy Herc while they anticipated the changes that were being implemented. Some of the changes would be transparent.

"Still punching out next month?" said Tumble.

"Yes sir. Did my duty and did enough. Getting out and going back to Texas. I'll join a legacy reserve 130 outfit and go to college. I have been accepted to start in the summer. I want to be a high school football coach, marry, raise children, and stay home," Hostile said.

"We will miss you. It is good to see you have a plan. Keep in touch and you can count on me for a recommendation. You can be proud of your Marine Corps service."

"Thank you, sir. I will be in touch."

"Bongo, try the Cheju ATIS. Find out what the weather is really like down there."

They listened through the static. The automatic terminal information service, ATIS, had mediocre news. There was light snow and a 1,500 feet ceiling. Visibility was okay. The problem was the wind. It was forty knots gusting higher and from the seaward side, the northwest. The wind was out of limits, very out of limits, for the long instrument runway. There was an answer. Shoot the approach to the instrument runway and circle just below the ceiling, maintain visual contact with the runway and land on the shorter runway into the wind. The winds around 1,500 feet would be higher than the surface winds and would push the circling Herc toward the rising terrain north of the shorter runway. The approach required a high angle of crab until the Herc was lined up into the wind where it would be okay.

"Ground contact, runway twelve o'clock," said Bongo.

Tumble had flown the precision ILS to the instrument runway with the significant crab angle required to maintain line up. Bongo made his call at 1,700 feet, a bit above forecast. Tumble stopped his descent at 1,220 feet MSL or 1,094 feet above the ground.

Tumble shifted his eyes from the instrument panel to outside the aircraft. He saw light blowing snow with clouds piled up against the 6,400 feet mountain. The peak was almost ten miles away but the steadily rising terrain started within a mile of the runway. The heavy snow clouds accumulated around the mountain bulked the appearance and made it appear closer. Tumble looked straight ahead at the instrument runway. He flew down it at 1,220 feet, crossed the landing runway intersection, extended than began his left circling turn keeping the landing runway in sight on his side of the Herc.

The Herc was configured at fifty flaps and landing gear down and flying at 150 knots indicated. The wind at their altitude was around 80 knots and the ground speed at 230 knots after they turned the corner to the downwind. The speed was pushing them toward the rising terrain.

Taking the excessive downwind speed into account Tumble started his turn to final at the abeam position. In the turn the wind, still pushing them away from the landing runway, became a high quartering tail wind, then a left to right cross wind to a front quartering wind, to a direct wind down the runway. It was all experienced skill to play it to make it with his angle of bank, speed and descent control. He knew the terrain was there. Bongo was visual out the right side and Rent had the radar up and was constantly monitoring their distance from the rising terrain and cross checking his tactical pilotage chart. Tumble fought the urge to look cross cockpit for a peek at the partially veiled mountain.

When hand flying in instrument conditions special care is required to not jerk the head about. The movement could induce vertigo or often the plane would follow the head shift and a small altitude hiccup could put it back into the overcast. That would require a missed approach maneuver and the execution of another approach. None of them wanted to do that.

Tumble could feel the Hercules aircraft buck as he turned crosswind and then, as the aircraft nose came into the wind, he felt the control forces required dampen and he knew his ground speed would decrease considerably with the wind in his face. He trimmed the nose for a touchdown at a thousand feet down the runway. He decided to stay with fifty flaps and use the reversible pitch props and the high head wind for the quick stop.

The touch-down was firm and on speed. Tumble took a deep breath but kept flying the wing until airspeed dissipated to a walk and he took over with the nose wheel steering. He taxied to the terminal where they had dropped the pheasant hunters on Monday. Tumble gave the command for engine shut down when the Korean lineman signaled they were in the correct parking position.

Bongo ran the checklist. The amber door open light came on as Hostile opened the main crew entrance door and stepped onto the ramp with the long interphone cord.

Tumble watched Hostile talk to a Korean man wearing a zippered, dark jacket, white shirt and dark tie. Hostile turned to face the cockpit, put open hands out from his side and shrugged his shoulders.

"Not here," Hostile said on the ICS.

"Damn," Bongo said.

"I know," Tumble said.

Tumble was not overly surprised but he had not believed the hunting party would not be present. The airplane had limited time on the ground. They had a primary mission to support the air group back in Japan; a group commanded by the pheasant hunting colonel. Tumble kicked himself. Despite the CO not giving him the traditional courtesy of a thank you when he disembarked Tumble knew he should have worked around the horse holder's maneuvers to keep them separated and spoken directly to the CO.

It took fifteen minutes to locate an airport employee who knew how to contact the Army recreation camp located on the far side of the mountain. He led them to a room with two chairs and two men. The men were smoking and drinking coffee. Despite the state of technology an old fashioned field phone sat on the floor between the two men. One man supervised while the other used the side crank to ring the camp. After several rings the phone was answered.

"This is Captain MacFarland. I am at the airport to pick up the Marine hunting party you have had there. Are they on the way to the airport?"

"No sir. They are in the field, hunting."

"Rough weather for that."

"Yes sir, but there are warming huts in the field. We are not expecting them back before supper time."

"Thanks soldier. Tell them their ride was here for the scheduled pickup."

Back at the Herc Tumble called for the checklists. After engine start he waited for Hostile to come aboard.

"Hostile, when we get to cruise I want a high frequency radio phone patch to squadron operations. They need to know about the no show."

A half hour later Tumble had his HF phone patch.

"Sailor, Tumble. The Cheju pheasant hunters are a no show. Don't know how they will be picked up. The point of contact blew me off. I told him several times when we would pick them up. They are out pheasant hunting."

"We have heavy maintenance here and the rest on the road. Don't have another Herc to send today. I'll talk to the CO. It's his boss pheasant hunting. He will want to have input. Phone patch me before you land and I will have the word for you."

"Roger that."

"Sergeant Lopez, terminate the phone patch. I will need another before we start descent," said Tumble.

The squadron was on the spot. Tumble knew that. Their own group exec as well as the fighter group commander needed to be picked up and he had an important training mission in conflict. He was cursing Ludlow aloud when Hostile gave him a cup of unrequested black coffee.

Tumble knew the answer before he heard it. Sailor passed the word that the CO wanted him to return to Cheju for the pick up on Friday. Get with the fighter guys and work something out. Magic would be needed.

The weather at Sakura was now about as bad as Cheju-do but there was only one runway. It was Bongo's leg and it would be a high, right to left, cross wind, precision, hand flown approach and landing. West and near to the runway was a high mountainous ridge line. The final approach controllers always gave a formulaic warning as they cleared aircraft for the approach.

"Rising terrain west of the airfield, do not fly west of the 240 degrees radial. You are cleared for the approach."

Aircraft on approach should not have to fly west of the 200 degree Sakura tacan radial but, close to the navigation aid, the emanated radials were physically close together and at 135 knots or more of ground speed it would not take much inattention to cross the forty radials and the consequences would be final. Bongo flew the precision instrument approach at Sakura. He made a text book cross wind approach and landing and congratulated himself all the way to parking.

As soon as the brakes were set and the door open the ops chief was up the ladder well with a message for Tumble to meet the fighter ops officer at the O Club. The night hops were a weather cancel.

Tumble was going to the O Club anyway for a plate of fried rice. Now he could have a beer with it. The night flights canceled the O Club was busier than a normal Thursday night. It took Tumble several minutes to locate Thor, the fighter operations officer.

Thor saw him coming and signaled the bartender for a beer. Without a word Thor handed the beer to Tumble.

Tumble nodded thanks and saluted with his beer.

"I know," Thor said. "I know."

"Hell of a way to run the air force," Tumble said.

"It'll work out. We were ahead on the quals and even with tonight gone we would have finished in three periods tomorrow."

"There is Saturday."

"If the weather breaks?"

"If it doesn't this won't look like the bull shit it is and we'll go with what we have."

They drank their beers in silence. Tumble ordered two more.

Chapter Eight Etai or It Hurts Good

Cold, moist air from the Pacific Ocean pushed over the warmer land as dawn approached. A sea fog formed. The mountains to the west of the sea and the air station fenced the dirty gray fog and the heavy organic scents of sea meeting land onto the sea side strip containing Marine Corps Air Station Sakura, Japan. The fog was a clinging wet sheath about all natural and man-made objects. A temperature drop of a few degrees would change the suspended moisture to freezing drizzle.

The takeoff was scheduled for late morning. The pheasant hunters would have the morning in the field. Evidently, the weather off the Yellow Sea and across Cheju-do was better than on the east coast of Japan. Tumble looked out the single window of his Bachelor Officers Quarters room. The cold, wet day was typical in mid winter. It was different from his permanent duty station on semi-tropical Okinawa where it would be wet and could be cold.

Dressed in shorts and tee shirt Tumble did stretches, sit ups, and pushups and the remainder of the daily seven for twenty minutes. Then, he sorted through his bag and came up with an out of fashion gray cotton sweat shirt with bold red USMC lettered on it and gray cotton sweat pants. He picked up his black, wool, watch cap and flight gloves. He would need them for his run.

Tumble stepped out the front door of the BOQ. The darkness of night was making a last stand. The streetlights and fog created pendants of alabaster shrouded light; from one light to the next gossamer strands reached out and touched the pavement where one circle, like frayed gauze, struggled to touch the next. The token haze of artificial light, in submission to the dying night, formed an ash gray coating over the deserted roads of the air station. The scents of residual diesel and jet exhaust and the faint, unique one from the nearby municipal crematorium mixed with the scent of thirty pounds of frying, mess hall bacon. He was use to them.

He began a slow run in the direction of the concrete and stone sea wall that ran between the air station and the sea. Atop the sea wall was a narrow road fully exposed to wind and sea spray. The paved road atop it ended at the Japanese military sea plane base where the big, amphibious, four engine, turbo prop Shin Maywa US-2 of the Japanese Maritime Self Defense Force was based. In the past summer one of the big search and rescue aircraft, flying from the auxiliary airfield on Iwo Jima, had landed in 10 foot seas to rescue a Marine Hornet pilot who had punched out two hundred miles east of Iwo Jima. Near the JMSDF base the road left the sea wall, ran parallel to the runway, and ended near a canal separating the base from an industrial area. A dirt and gravel patrol road picked up at the canal and crossed the approach end of runway 20 to continue past the fighter side of the air station where the Hornets, in lethal beauty, sat. The paved road picked back up and wound past the golf course and the base theater before passing an old Zero hangar cum garden shed and ending at the BOQ start point. It was a good, long running route, perhaps seven miles if a zigzag or two was thrown in.

The distance from the BOQ to the sea wall ramp was over a flat, paved half mile. Tumble needed the distance to get into the rhythm of the run. He pushed up the ramp and glanced at the gray and black sea sparsely topped with light reflecting, startling white, silver rimmed, foam. The waves rolled and crashed into the sea wall filling the air with spray and mist. Tumble could taste the salt spray. The intensity of the sea noise surprised him and broke his concentration. The prolific sea bed kelp was blacker than the dark sea. The surge and ebb of breakers against the concrete slabs of sea wall transformed the broad leaves of the kelp into a many tentacled and unknown sea beast grasping upward at the land, at him.

Atop the sea wall Tumble paused and inhaled the rich vichyssoise of the pungent scents of sea weed, and fish, and life in a land far from his home. The cold and wet dampened the scents and they were not the overpowering, hearty stew of odors of the hot tropical seas. The sharpness of the strange land's sights and scents and the wet and cold and the exertion of his running made him notice the feel of life coursing his veins. His smile was a straight line with the corners turned up.

Life as he now knew it was flying, myriad military duties, Officers Club, and one more country song on the juke box. It was a lonely life. It had not always been so. There was no relief in sight.

Tumble lowered his head and ran. The light wind was steady and served to stir and deepen the sea fog. Despite the low temperature and wind he could feel himself sweating and it was good.

"You may think it funny when you see a Japanese western movie and the cowboy is wounded as he will say 'etai' and that is Japanese for 'it hurts good', " the captain at Quantico had said to the officer candidates. "When you hurt here or anywhere in training, remember, 'etai', it hurts good. Now, let me hear you say it." The captain had walked away leaving them to the sergeants' tender mercies and screaming "etai" at the top of their lungs. It worked though. When Tumble pushed himself to the point of pain or exhaustion he would think, "etai." He had not thought to ask any of the Japanese he had met if the story was true.

The fog became a lighter gray, not thinner, just a subtle color change with the sun rising higher from the sea, the land of the rising sun. At the end of the sea wall Tumble angled left on a paved road that took him past the sea plane base. He could see the shadow form of a giant rescue aircraft the Shin Maywa US-2 flying boat that had replaced the older Shin Miewa US-1A. The indistinct, fog wrapped shadow blurred the silhouette and a small boy's mind would have seen a giant science fiction animal rising from a 1950's Tokyo Bay.

The breathing sounds were quick and without the steady rhythm of a runner settled in stride. Tumble heard an unintelligible comment. He glanced over his right shoulder and saw two runners materialize from the fog. Their compact litheness identified them as Japanese. He increased his pace a step as the two runners came along side. They formed on his right and nodded a greeting.

In silence, the trio covered another mile at a seven and a half minute pace. Then, still silent, their muscles and joints warm and flowing in smooth motion, The Japanese runners increased their speed. Tumble was feeling good and matched their stride. He knew he was not a fast runner, eight minutes a mile all day, seven minutes for seven, and maybe two miles at six minutes, maybe.

He would stay with these two for as long as he could. Perhaps they would have to stay with him. At the canal they cut back around the end of the runway on the dirt perimeter road. The pace increased again though none could have said who stepped it up.

The thick fog and their sweat soaked them. Their breathing was steady and deep. The cold air was invigorating, a source of energy drawn deep into their lungs. Tumble felt the hot mucous from his nose form cold and flowing on his upper lip. It was what happened when he ran in the cold and wet, a social faux pau if mentioned in polite company. When he could no longer bear it he wiped his nose with the sleeve of his sweat shirt. As was their custom his fellow runners pretended to not have seen the motion. Soon, their turn would come. They ran in an opaque world. Vision faded to nothing at two hundred feet. Their runner rhythm, breathing, and the muffled break of the sea on the now distant sea wall were the only sounds.

Tumble noticed his leg weariness; his lungs needed more oxygen. The man to his immediate right sensed it and kicked up the pace as they approached the golf course. Tumble matched him. The other man lost a half step.

Tumble decided to bluff. He had been running further than the other two and would stop at the BOQ. He knew where his race would end and they did not. He kicked to his best, a six minute pace. Off to the far left was the golf course club house and, to his right, faintly visible, was the huge red letter, neon sign of the station theater.

The lead Japanese runner seemed to know the race would soon end. He knew they were approaching the BOQ area. Tumble saw the man's knees come up higher, his stride lengthen and hit a five and a half minute pace. Tumble had never been there. He pushed himself. His eyes closed to slits, his head came back, his mouth opened wider to ram air into his lungs, and his hot, exhaled breath cut a track across his freezing upper lip.

Now the sounds were heavy breathing and running feet on black top. The tennis courts went by on the left, and past them, on the right, the old Zero aircraft hangar, now a lawn mower utility shed.

They made a sharp left at the intersection. Behind them were the main gate and the town. The BOQ office and the Officers Club were the next landmarks.

"O Club," Tumble said.

There was an answering grunt. The front runner understood. The race would end there. The other man sounded a step behind and pushing hard. Tumble was running faster than he ever had. He did not have enough air; his vision narrowed. He could hear blood pumping through his veins and feel the surge of his heart.

Passing the Officers Club Tumble was a half a heart beat behind the lead runner. He broke stride fast, stumbled, and almost fell. All three runners slowed to a jog.

Tumble started to walk. The first place Japanese runner circled back to Tumble, smiled and looked him in the eyes. Tumble returned the look and gave a thumbs up.

"Banzai," said Tumble and "etai," he thought.

"Oooorah," said the Japanese runner.

Tumble extended his hand. The two Japanese runners shook his hand. They turned and resumed their run at a slower pace.

Tumble was physically hurting, chest heaving for air, yet mentally he felt great. It had been a perfect run. He cooled down several more minutes and walked back to the BOQ. He entered the warm lobby and noticed the vapor rise from his wet clothing. The temperature contrast was stifling and he felt queasy. He had not eaten and he wanted a cup of coffee. He would wait for the coffee and drink it at the flight line.

In his room he stripped down and turned on the shower. He started the water cool and then ran it hot. He felt the soothing water pour over his body and relax his muscles. He soaped and shampooed and rinsed with the water as hot as he could take it. He ran the water to cold, placed both hands against the tile shower wall and stood with the water beating against the top of his head. He thought about the weather, the flight, the canceled training, the upcoming ops, his estranged wife and dead son.

Tumble roughly toweled himself and sat nude and hair damp on the government issued desk chair in his room. The thin damp towel was draped across his lap.

"The Marine Corps and flying, all I have. A lousy life but a great job," he said to no one. It sounded self pitying and he knew it.

Chapter Nine Chilled Pheasant

Frontal activity brought higher, gusting winds ashore with rain and overcast skies. The morning fog was gone and the temperature stayed above freezing. Tumble walked to the flight line for his first cup of coffee. It would be chow hall coffee from a two gallon insulated jug. Coffee tasted better outdoors.

The yellow light was on above the aircraft maintenance office door. It gave off a fuzzy yellow halo that pushed against the dreary daylight

"Good morning, Top Halsey," Tumble said to the squadron maintenance chief.

"Same to you, Captain," said Master Sergeant Halsey.

"Thanks."

He was early but the Top was ready. He always was. Tumble reviewed the aircraft log book. It looked good enough to go. He called base ops and talked to the weather guesser. Icing passing a thousand feet and weather worsening the rest of the day was the best guess. Rent would stop by for the formal brief. He told the Top he was going to the airplane. He looked past the lit cigarette in the Top's hand.

He could hear the rumble of a diesel power cart and smell the exhaust before he could see the yellow machine. He ignored the shallow, dirty, pad eye puddles with the rainbow sheen of waste oil. He walked to the crew entrance door on the forward left side of the KC-130 Hercules. He let himself in and stored his just-in-case bag under the aluminum can shaped 3,600 gallon internal fuselage fuel tank.

Next, he climbed the short ladder to the flight deck and braced himself at the top of the ladder. He spoke to Rodeo who was in the flight engineer seat running preflight checks. At the top of the ladder was a hinged galley deck that could be dropped into place during flight. With his legs across the gap, four feet above the level of the cargo deck, he depressed the insulated jug spigot and helped himself to the anticipated cup of black coffee. Perhaps not the best roast but it was good when fresh and strong.

Tumble carefully worked his way down the ladder and out of the Herc. He ignored the light drizzle. He held a cup of very hot coffee in a Victor china mug with a squadron insignia on one side and his name on the other. The coffee made a small hot pool and from that black pool heat rose, collided with the cool air and formed a small layer of fog across the top of the coffee that lifted into the air and was visible four inches above the cup. He shivered in the damp chill, inhaled the aroma and drank the hot black coffee. He felt the caffeine effect and his general outlook improved. He smiled to himself thankful that the air station mess sergeant had not taken the order, to make weaker coffee for the modern taste, to heart. Some of the best coffee he had tasted had come fresh and hot from the chow hall and some of the worst, too. He took a second sip and looked to the sky. The rain and clouds restricted his vision. Despite the forecast Tumble strained his eyes for an improvement in the weather. It was habitual with the profession. His automatic concern was rewarded by light cold drizzle on his face.

The squadron commanding officer, Lieutenant Colonel Hitchkok, was in a bind with the training and the pheasant hunters. Someone had promised too much but no one was willing to call things off because that would mean telling the group CO bad news. There were too many fitness reports riding on this and the bet was it would come out in the wash.

Now, the tanker qualification hops for the day were officially canceled due to weather. His Herc was available without conflict. The situation was no longer a wash. Tumble was now an official jerk and without a viable excuse because of his insistence on the Thursday pheasant hunter pickup. The only potential good news was that the horse holder had, most likely, not mentioned the problem to the air group CO.

None of it mattered as Tumble knew he was already high on Wild Bill Hitchkok's shit list. Just before Thanksgiving he had loaded a six pack pickup truck and five marines to take from Okinawa to Pohang, Korea. The weather had been lousy.

Pohang airfield is on the east coast of Korea. The instrument runway, parallel to the sea, is good but it is at the bottom of a three sided bowl of rocks. Half a nautical mile off the approach end of the instrument runway is a ridge over three hundred feet above the approach end runway elevation. West of the airfield and close is rugged terrain that rises steadily to over two-thousand feet above the airport elevation. Several years prior the Marine Corps had lost a Ch-53 Sea Stallion, killing 22 out of 37 marines, in the mountainous region around Pohang.

The available approach is a tacan non-precision approach. On the final approach the aircraft is at a minimum descent altitude of 660 feet or 590 feet above the touchdown zone elevation when it crosses the 315 feet high ridge on the extended runway centerline, a lot of altitude to dump in close during instrument conditions. The aircraft is at a speed around 135 knots at that point and, if the runway is in sight by the missed approach point, the Herc pilot will drop the flaps to one hundred or full flaps and let the nose rotate sharply down and keep it pointed at the painted runway numbers to land in the first thousand feet or less of the runway. Lots of Pohang runway should be left for the reversible Hamilton Standard props to stop the big Hercules aircraft.

If the runway is not in sight for a stabilized maneuver to land then the pilot executes the missed approach procedure. The missed approach maneuver calls for a near maximum power increase, military power, a rotation of the aircraft to a positive angle of climb, 5 to 7 degrees nose up and wings level, and a 65 degrees turn to pick up a 30 degrees heading to intercept the 10 degree radial outbound to a holding point over the open sea and away from the rocks and hills. The climb is continued to 5,000 feet. The approach may then be repeated.

Failure to properly execute the missed approach maneuver can have immediate and unhealthy consequences. Straight ahead on the runway heading the terrain quickly rises to 800 feet. There is choppy high terrain all about and it rises over 2,000 feet within 25 miles of the airfield. Perfect situational awareness is required at all times. The Marine legacy KC-130's primary source for positioning is the onboard navigational instrument the tacan or tactical air navigation system. The instrument rotating needle, centered on a compass card, denotes radial from and bearing to a charted ground tacan station. Distance from the station is slant range and is referred to as DME, distance measuring equipment, and is used as nautical miles. The closer the aircraft is to the ground the closer the slant range comes to actual horizontal distance.

There are limitations and tacan reliability can vary with a variety of factors. The ground station needs maintenance, the onboard equipment or antennae may need adjustment, atmospheric conditions have occasional adverse affect and the signal can be attenuated or blocked by terrain. Tacan equipment is susceptible to the electronic deception or meaconing that occurs on a semi-regular basis on the Korean peninsula. Problems can't always be pin pointed or deception quickly recognized. If the pilot feels a mental pinch, suspects something undefined is not right, the pilot should respect that suspicion.

Tumble had felt the start of a pinch. The ground controller had given them holding instructions at 5,000 feet on the final approach course. A U.S Air Force C-130 was shooting the tacan approach. The controller stated the weather at the exact minimums of 600 feet ceiling and one and a half miles horizontal visibility. Weather is rarely exactly at minimums. When it is called that way it is often code for take a look, maybe you will break out for the landing.

Tumble monitored the Air Force C-130 through four approaches. On each approach the Herc failed to see the runway and executed a missed approach to a radar pick up for vectors back around for another try.

In the holding pattern over the final approach course Tumble watched the tacan needle on his instrument panel. The needle was coupled to needles on the horizontal situation indicator, HSI, and gave him his position relative to course and on the same instrument, behind the needles, was his primary attitude indicator which enabled him to keep right side up in the goo. The primary tacan needle was breaking lock and spinning 360 degrees on a regular basis before locking back onto the signal. The HSI course deviation indicator bounced erratically five to ten degrees or full deflection either side of the selected course. It was good to be above the terrain and over the sea.

Tumble listened to the conversation between the approach controller and the Air Force pilot and the pilot was not complaining about the tacan signal. Tumble suspected the problem was on board his aircraft though he had not experienced any enroute tacan difficulties. Maybe the Air Force C-130 had a different model tacan or the antennas were located differently from his. Any of those variables could make a difference and Tumble's confidence factor in his equipment was eroded.

The Air Force C-130 went missed approach for the fifth time and enough was enough. The Air Force pilot requested clearance to Osan Air Base, not that the weather was better there, but Osan had a precision approach that provided course and glide slope guidance with a DH (decision height) of 200 feet above the ground and the surrounding terrain was flat. Tumble considered asking the Air Force pilot about his tacan signal reception but decided against it as the guy was up to his eye balls in alligators and would not care to chat.

"I'm no better instrument pilot than the Air Force pilot and I think our tacan is shaky. Tell the controller we want to go to Osan, too," Tumble said.

Bongo worked it out with the controller and away they went. On the way Tumble called the sergeant in charge of the truck marines to the flight deck and told him the weather and equipment issue.

They would wait, at Osan, for the weather to improve and try again. When Tumble could not give him a time or even assurance it would be that day the sergeant said he was familiar with the roads between Osan and Pohang and he needed to be in Pohang. Therefore, he would drive there.

When they checked in back home on the squadron frequency the duty lieutenant told Tumble the CO wanted to see him as soon as he landed. Tumble knew an unpleasant conversation was coming. The squadron CO had promised his boss, the group CO, that the sergeant with his marines and truck would be delivered to Pohang. That had not happened.

Tumble still had a vivid memory of the conversation. Wild Bill had met him in the passage way of the hangar quarterdeck area.

"I understand you did not try the approach, Captain."

"Yes sir, my tacan was bouncing around, the weather was at minimums and the Air Force 130 in front of me had not made it in five tries. I decided the smart thing to do was to wait."

"You did not try. I always give it a shot. Of course, you are to err on the side of safety, considering all factors including the aircraft and your personal competence."

"Under the circumstances I wasn't sure we could take a safe shot. Sometimes one is all you get."

"You have an instrument rating, Captain. Do not confuse demanding with unsafe," said Wild Bill as he turned and walked away.

Tumble had seen the spark of anger in Wild Bill's eyes. He thought of all the times he had heard Wild Bill and others say, "there's not a war on. No reason to take unnecessary chances. Fly safe and live to fly another day. Make the right decision."

Perhaps, if the decision embarrasses the CO, it is not the right decision. So, here he was, on the way to Cheju-do after once again irritating his CO.

"Enough navel gazing," said Tumble.

"What?" Said Bongo.

"Check list," said Tumble.

They ran the checks down to engine start as they waited for Rent, the navigator, to return from base operations.

Tumble listened to the current tower weather. The winds were gusting well out of limits for takeoff. He asked the tower controller about interval between gusts, not that it was a predictor. He was stalling his decision. The wind was hitting

45 knots at 90 degrees to the runway. Not a smart decision to takeoff. The CO wanted the pheasant hunters picked up and he would be extremely unhappy if Tumble did not make the trip.

"Lousy weather everywhere," said Rent. "The weather won't get better today. Winds won't drop until late tonight and marginal weather tomorrow. Maybe we'll get the training hops out and maybe not. It has to be clear on top to refuel. Could be Sunday flying in our future."

"Yeah, flexibility, and we're going to Cheju-do," said Tumble.

It had not been a decision until he heard himself say it. As he voiced the decision Tumble felt the ice maker in his stomach dump in cold cubes of apprehension. It was a wrong decision for wrong reasons.

The correct decision was to delay or cancel the flight. The winds were gusting well outside the aircraft performance limits. Publically the CO would accept that. He had to, but after the Pohang truck conversation Tumble knew the CO would write him off as a non hacker, failed to complete another assigned mission, one personally important to the CO and the CO's career, lack of loyalty on Tumble's part. Tumble knew he already would be fortunate to get a no harm fitness report from Wild Bill. He was past getting a good one.

Tumble looked out from the silent flight deck. No one spoke. He called the tower for a wind update.

"Winds from 110 degrees, 30 knots, gusts 45 knots," the tower voice said.

"Shouldn't be a problem getting out between gusts," said Tumble.

"Okay," Bongo said. He smiled and dribbled snuff into his foam cup.

Tumble was wrong. The 45 plus knots gusts, two quick ones rocked the Herc just after rotation as the landing gear was coming up. The Herc was around a hundred feet above the ground. The control inputs were in for a cross wind takeoff, wing down into the wind and opposite rudder. Still, the Herc rolled sharply to the edge of flight control authority. Tumble extended his leg for full rudder deflection. He lifted his right hand from the throttles and, with both hands on the horns of the control yoke, twisted the yoke past 90 degrees of rotation to full deflection of the hydraulically actuated ailerons putting the wing full into the wind. The gusts dropped. The flight control input was too much. He over corrected the Herc around the longitudinal axis. Momentarily, he was wall to wall with flight controls and the Herc wildly rocked. Passing 300 feet the Herc was stable. The flight deck was silent.

Gear and flaps up, lights retracted and off, climb checks complete, and the Herc above 10,000 feet Tumble passed control of the aircraft to Bongo. At cruise altitude Tumble left the seat and went to the galley for a cup of coffee.

Rent was there putting the galley deck in place. He poured them each a cup. He did not speak. He arched his eyebrows at Tumble.

"If we had lost an engine I'm not sure I could have put us back in, Rent."

"Never heard anyone say that before. They probably should have."

Tumble turned away and bumped against Hostile, the loadmaster, and dribbled coffee on both of them. He automatically apologized and returned to his seat. No one spoke to him.

He could not put himself in a good light no matter how he twisted the facts. He had risked his aircraft and crew because he was concerned about his fitness report. It was a bad decision. He was angry with himself. He vowed over and over to himself to never again let career influence a safety of flight decision.

The weather was better at Cheju-do. There was enough overcast to require a precision instrument approach. It would be straight in so there would be no circling toward high terrain.

The landing was uneventful. Tumble taxied the Herc toward the military passenger area. He could see the pheasant hunters milling about. He parked, set the brakes, and directed the shutdown of the Allison engines. He kept the self contained auxiliary power unit running. Hostile opened the ramp and aft cargo door for easier loading. There were several white, plastic wrapped boxes stacked in obvious preparation for loading onto the Herc. Those would be boxes of chilled pheasant.

Lieutenant Colonel Ludlow was up the flight deck ladder before Tumble was out of the seat.

"Captain, heard you were here yesterday," Ludlow said.

Tumble saw a man with a sandlot car salesman look on his face and the look read: "You are screwed and I am not."

"Yes sir, just as I told you."

"The hunt always goes through Friday, Captain, just as I told you. It is all flight time anyway," Ludlow said and he showed a lot of teeth with his winners grin.

"No, it is not," said Tumble. He deliberately dropped the sir. He ignored Ludlow's outstretched hand.

"Captain, I understand why you pilots get flight pay. I don't understand why you get officer pay."

Tumble did not trust himself to say another word. He noticed Hostile was back on the flight deck for the weight and balance Form 365. He was not sure how long Hostile had been there but from the look of it Tumble thought Hostile had heard the short and hard conversation between the two officers.

Tumble went to the back of the Herc and watched the loading. The boxes were packed with ice and dead pheasants. He noticed brown corrugated boxes containing grandfather clocks and a roll top desk. The Korean craftsmen were good at producing such items in local cottage industry. They made them in components suitable for easy shipping or loading through an aircraft door.

Standing on the airport ramp Tumble watched as Ludlow walked over to the group commander standing on the concrete outside the passenger area. He watched Ludlow in conversation with the group CO, saw them turn in his direction and laugh, enjoying a private joke. Hostile was standing near them, waiting for a break in the conversation, to inform them it was time to come aboard.

Once at cruise altitude Tumble asked for a high frequency radio phone patch to the weather forecasters at Sakura. The winds were out of limits with peak gusts even higher than at takeoff. The winds were not forecast to decrease for several hours. No one was flying.

"Rent, work out a flight plan from overhead Sakura back to Okinawa. We'll check the winds overhead Sakura. If they are still up we'll divert to the Rock. Have to land at the 24 our ops Air Force base. It will be too late to get home. We'll fly out from Okinawa tomorrow and meet the fighters on track."

"I'm on it, Tumble."

"Hostile, ask Lieutenant Colonel Ludlow to come to the flight deck."

Ludlow arrived on the flight deck seemingly pleased and no longer interested in being well met. His expression changed as Tumble outlined his decision.

"Captain, we are from Marine Corps Air Station Sakura and we want to go back to Sakura. The group CO has work to do there; not on Okinawa."

"I understand that, sir. I will try to make that happen. My final decision will be made overhead Sakura and it will be a safety of flight decision."

"Just make the right one, Captain. Your group XO is on this trip and will not be pleased if this flight is not completed as planned."

"Yes sir. Sergeant Lopez, phone patch to squadron ops. They will want a heads up on the potential divert."

"That is your decision and your responsibility, Captain," said Ludlow.

"I never doubted it," Tumble said and dropped the "sir".

Ludlow left the flight deck. He looked like the boy at school who was going to tattle.

"Absolute idiot," said Bongo. The voice was conversational. He ran his tongue through the snuff between his lip and his teeth. He sipped his coffee.

"Absolute idiot," Bongo repeated sotto voce as he stared out the side swing window.

Tumble ignored the remark. He doubted anyone else had heard it and he was in no mood to reprimand Bongo.

Approaching Sakura at cruise altitude Bongo completed the formality of confirming the bad news. Tumble knew the landing was possible, just not smart. The landing was possible if the Herc was flown with a high degree of skill and asymmetrical power application from the high, wing mounted turboprops and a dollop of luck. Perhaps it was a landing to be attempted before running out of ideas and airspeed at the same time and with no place left to go. They had plenty of gas and plenty of options. Why try this landing? High winds, out of limit winds, varying 70 to 90 degrees to the runway presented a degree of risk considerably above normal. Tumble recalled the wind conditions at takeoff.

The flight overflew Sakura and landed at Okinawa Air Force Base where there were around the clock operations. They parked at the Navy transit line. They would takeoff Saturday in time to meet the fighters on track.

A second Marine KC-130 was on the line with two engines running. Tumble watched Wild Bill approach his aircraft. He did not come to the flight deck. He went to the back and escorted the passengers to the running Herc. Marines transferred the boxed pheasants, grandfather clocks, and roll top desk to the other Herc.

Bongo signaled Tumble to put on his headset. It was Sailor Mann calling from the other aircraft on the squadron UHF frequency.

"We are taking them back tonight, Tumble," said Sailor. "I will fly a long, slow dog leg. The winds should be in limits by the time we get there. As long as these guys are moving they will be happy. Tumble, good luck."

Wild Bill, the squadron CO, stood on the flight line and watched Sailor taxi. He turned and walked back to Tumble's aircraft.

Rodeo had turned on the white cockpit dome lights to flood the cockpit with bright light. Sergeant Hostile Lopez was putting his paper work together at the rear of the cockpit when the CO came up the ladder well.

Lopez was the first man the CO saw. The CO was carrying his head cover in his right hand. Without a word the CO used his cover to slap Sergeant Lopez. Lopez turned his head in surprise and shock. Twice more, with his cover, the CO slapped Lopez on the back of the head.

"You need a haircut. You need a haircut. You flew the group XO and you need a haircut. You flew the fighter group CO and you need a haircut. Be in my office at 0800 and have a haircut," said the CO.

Tumble and the others on the flight deck were stunned and immobilized. Tumble looked at Lopez. He could not see that Lopez was in need of a haircut but Lopez was flushed red, fists clenched, and holding back words and tears of anger.

The CO turned to Tumble. He poked his forefinger against Tumble's chest.

"You are responsible, Captain. He is your responsibility. The crew is your responsibility. You are to ensure your crew look like marines," said the CO as he used his forefinger against Tumble's chest to emphasize each bullet point.

The angry CO turned and was gone before Tumble recovered enough for a formulaic, "yes sir."

Tumble placed his hand on Hostile's shoulder. He was at a loss for words.

"I'll handle this, sir. I'll see that Sergeant Lopez is ready to report to the CO at 0800," said Rodeo.

The CO did not see Sergeant Hostile Lopez the next morning. The squadron sergeant major was waiting for him and he talked to Lopez in the privacy of his office.

Sergeant Lopez did not return to Sakura with the crew. He was returned early to MCAS World for his scheduled discharge. Sergeant Enrique "Hostile" Lopez had honorably completed his United States Marine Corps enlistment. Tumble did not see Hostile again.

Chapter Ten Horse Dancing

It was Bongo's turn to fly. He was in the left seat. They came in for the Sakura break, the Air Force called the maneuver a pitch out, and it was the quickest way to maneuver the aircraft for landing in clear weather. They had left Okinawa late afternoon to arrive on the tanker track near Sakura. The Hornets had met them to continue the weather interrupted training.

Bongo overflew the runway at 1,500 feet and 250 knots and, at the upwind numbers, rolled the Herc level and right into a 45 degrees angle of bank turn over Sakura Bay. He pulled the four throttles to flight idle. Tumble was prepared for that and held his finger on the gear warning horn button to keep it from blaring when the throttles came back. They dirtied on speed, fifty flaps at 180 knots, landing gear down at 170 knots. By the abeam position the aircraft was configured for approach and the speed was coming back. Bongo looked out cross cockpit at the intended point of landing, continued descent, flew on several seconds and then started a 180 degree turn to final at 30 degrees angle of bank. He set the throttles to maintain 2,500 inch pounds of torque on each engine and slowed to the final approach speed. A half nautical mile, 3,000 feet horizontal from landing he had the Herc 200 feet above the sea. He called for 100 flaps. The additional drag caused by the big fowler flaps coming full down slowed the Herc and rolled the nose over. Bongo trimmed for landing and flared to touchdown. They taxied in and parked abeam three other squadron tankers parked on the flight line for the operation.

"O Club," said Bongo.

"Meet you there. I'm going by the Q."

Tumble had mail to read. He had left an unopened letter from his ex's lawyer, or soon to be ex, on the dresser. When he reached the BOQ and looked at the envelope he decided to put off reading the letter. Bad news could wait. He washed his face, brushed the coffee off his teeth, put a fresh tee shirt on under his flight bag, and walked across the street to the Officers Club.

It was after 1800 when Tumble walked into a crowded O Club. The fighter pilots, who had completed their quals, were deep into tension release and animal acts were out of the cage. The presence of Navy nurses, DOD school teachers, a couple of wives, and a few free spirited bar girls on their night off heightened the feeding frenzy. Slipping through the atmosphere on tendrils of laughter was oldie but gold rock music from a live Filipino band at the far end of the room away from the long bar. The band sounded like the originals.

The tanker pilots had the visitors area staked out. It was the small portion of bar near the bad luck table above which hung a plaque holding a bent propeller from a C-12 twin engine turboprop aircraft. The prop tips at 90 degrees to the blade were the results of a gear up landing. The fighter pilots rarely had a recognizable piece big enough for a wall plaque when their luck went south for the winter.

Scoping the dimly lit room and looking at the dance floor Tumble saw Wild Bill had managed to corner a school teacher. Her nails were too long for a Navy nurse. The teacher was at least fifteen years younger than Wild Bill and good looking with short dark hair, tanned, fit and wearing red trolling heels. She would have Wild Bill turning into a wedge, simplest tool known to man, and hand walking on the dance floor if she did not dump him for a fighter lieutenant in ten minutes. Either way it would be entertaining. Giving him his due Tumble knew Wild Bill could be smooth and personable.

Don Juan and Bongo anchored the tanker end of the bar. Tumble walked over and they made room for him. He leaned against the bar facing the dance floor. Without a word of greeting Bongo handed him a beer and indicated another on the bar. He was behind again. Juan was suffering post Australia, love sick blues and, as befitting his professional status, big annual bonus, and place of birth immediately west of the Florida panhandle, he was drinking call bourbon up and water back.

The first sip of hoppy beer was cold past the teeth and on the tongue, the coolness rising and filling his mouth. The taste was crisp and distinct. The first beer was the best beer. It always was. He could stop. He knew he would not. He would have a few more beers. The discipline required to mentally compartmentalize was not constant. If a man could not mope when he was drinking beer then when could he mope?

The letter at the BOQ was not from his ex wife. It was from her lawyer. He wondered about her. Where was she? What was she doing? Was she seeing someone? The letter was, most likely, clean up paperwork needing a signature. It had the makings of a bad country song.

Bongo was mesmerized by the pretty DOD school teacher laughing with Wild Bill. The girl had a clear lilt to her voice and an easy laugh. She was use to being pretty, use to being the bell of the frat parties, use to being the prettiest in the room, use to special attention. This situation looked no different to her. She had dated professors as old as the pilot talking to her. She knew how to keep an entertaining line coming while being available for better. She glanced about and saw Bongo's interest and Tumble's non interest. She filed the information under maybe.

Tumble saw the girl smile at Bongo and Bongo smile back.

"Don't try it partner. You will just piss off the CO. He is playing lieutenant tonight," said Tumble.

"Free fighter," said Bongo.

"Not tonight. Wild Bill is drinking himself young, not stupid. Tomorrow will come and you will still be the third lieutenant on the right and he will be your commanding officer."

"Wasn't the old west gunfighter's name Hickok, not Hitchkok?" said Bongo.

"Don't go there."

Around 1930, 7:30 p.m. world time, the pupu table was down to greasy, potato chip crumbs, wizened broccoli, and the dried remnants of onion dip. The band switched effortlessly to country music. The night could go either way. It could roll over and quit or boom. No flying was scheduled for Sunday.

The heads, restrooms, were against a side wall half way down the room. There was a tall, lattice work, wood screen in front of the doors. Feminine squeals and male shouts of laughter sounded and the crowd recoiled from the area near the wood screen. It was the Red Sea parting, swirling, making an opening, and refilling the void, moving across the room. In the swirl was a cleared circle and in the space was a fighter pilot. The identification was possible because there was an amateur marker made tattoo of pilot wings and a fighter squadron patch on the left cheek of his buttocks. The left cheek was visible because the fighter pilot was wearing flight boots, a jock strap, and red thong panties over his head. He was running with an awkward gait explained by the need to keep his gluteus muscles clinched in order to hold the flaming tail of brown paper towels in place. He held his arms swept back and he turned and soared as a jet in flight.

"Burner, burner, afterburner," chanted the other fighter pilots as they reeled back clearing the area around their flaming squadron mate.

He was near flameout when he reached back and grabbed the lit paper towel tail. His clothed wingman handed him a shot glass of 151 rum. His buddies knew what was coming. Those between him and the squadron wall plaque jumped to the side or dropped to the floor dragging the slow with them.

The fighter pilot lifted enough red thong to expose his mouth. He threw his head back while sloshing the rum in his mouth. He held the flaming paper towel arms length in front of his face and sprayed the high test rum, in a fine mist, through the paper towel sourced flame. The flame changed from yellow and flashed to blue then leapt the three feet to the squadron wall plaque, a baptism of fire. The semi-nude fighter pilot ran from the room, gone quicker than he had come. A protective crowd closed behind him.

Tumble and Bongo stood watching with their backs to the bar. Juan had kept his face to the bar like a love sick fifteen year old. Wild Bill and the school teacher were standing arms length in front of them. They each had one arm around the waist of the other and were pressed full length side to side.

Bongo could not move his eyes from the girl. She was a few inches over five feet, petite athletic figure, and naturally shapely legs enhanced by exercise. She was wearing an electric blue slip dress. Tumble thought his wife might have described it as periwinkle. The dress was fashionably tight and when she stood on tip toe her dress levitated inches up her thighs. Past the odors of alcohol and churning, sweating bodies the scent of her perfume, not floral but a distinctive, alluring, subtle musk reached Bongo.

The look, the perfume, the beer was more than Bongo could handle. He reached his hand out, palm up, grabbed and squeezed a handful of beautifully accentuated, curved buttocks.

The girl squealed in surprise. She struggled to turn in the tight crowd. Her eyes flashed with anger. She sought vengeance. Bongo had his back to her and appeared to be in conversation with the Japanese bartender. Tumble stood stunned, mouth agape, a beer in his left hand, his right hand partially open and extended where he had, too late, reached to stop Bongo.

The girl pursed her mouth, stared Tumble in the eye, and cocked a fist past her ear. She brought the fist through a strengthening arc straight to Tumble's jaw. The sound was distinct, unmistakable, sharp, and relayed the extent of the force exerted, flesh striking flesh. Tumble felt his knees tremble and his vision narrow. He felt Don Juan's helping hand on his back and right elbow and he was barely able to maintain his upright position.

Wild Bill saw the hit. He was unsure what had happened but he gave Tumble a contemptuous grin that promised more and turned his attention back to the girl.

Bongo stopped his fake conversation with the bar tender. Juan was amused and ordered a bourbon up and water back for Tumble. Tumble skipped the water.

Wild Bill escorted the girl to the squadron table and ordered four pizzas for his pilots sans the two at the bar. He looked at Tumble, whispered to the girl and laughed. She did not laugh. She was still seething.

"Thanks, partner," Tumble said.

"Anytime," said Bongo. He signaled for another round.

Somewhere in the developing evening maelstrom the fighter pilots began a horseback dancing contest. Nurses, school teachers, two wives, and a Filipino waitress were hoisted atop pilot shoulders. The dancers spun and gyrated and danced in time to the tunes.

Wild Bill hesitated but his school teacher had signed up for the full experience. It was her first big night at the O Club. She prodded and pulled at him until he found his knees on the sticky, damp floor. She climbed on a chair, hiked her dress to a freedom of movement level and mounted his shoulders spilling her umbrella vodka drink down Wild Bill's back in the process.

It was a breath taking view. Wild Bill rose with the strength of ten and joined the younger pilots on the dance floor.

Someone pried Wild Bill's right hand from a grip high on the girl's thigh. They replaced the warm flesh with a cold beer. He looked as if he could use it. A drink with a tumbling fruit salad was thrust toward the girl. She shifted position to take it and put a question to rest. The shift exposed a tiny ribbon of black lace.

Tumble looked. It was a view hard to miss. He had been wronged and with each swallow of beer his mind had taken leave of caution and good sense. The moving, beautiful, mostly bare, feminine derriere presented itself scant inches from his face. With a fool's courage he playfully but firmly bit the right cheek of that which was exposed before him.

The girl yelped and lunged forward pounding her full weight against the back of Wild Bill's head. Wild Bill now had a center of gravity shift and it was out of limits. The two tall, too tall couple fell forward into the crush of horseback dancers dragging horseback couple after horseback couple down in a chain reaction that reached across the dance floor.

Tumble, Bongo, and Don Juan turned to face the bar. Their backs were to the dance floor though all was visible in the mirror behind the bar. Bongo signaled the Japanese bartender for another round. He left a twenty dollar tip as hush money.

Chapter Eleven The East Sea

The Sea of Japan Operations were underway. The first flights had gone without a problem if C2, Crazy Calvin, was not counted. C2 was the tanker squadron executive officer, the XO, the second in command. He had been fetched from Okinawa. He was taking Wild Bill's flights for the week.

Wild Bill had sprained his right wrist and jammed the fingers of his right hand in the Saturday night dance floor fall. The finger joints were swollen and stiff and the fingers looked like big andouille sausages. The skin covering them was a dark red quickly turning a purple and yellow hue. Nothing official would be done as there was too much blame to go around and witnesses to what exactly had happened were not reliable. No one stepped forward to say who had nipped the school teacher and she was no longer sure it had been a nip or, at least, that was the way she was playing it. Don Juan summed it up as, "alcohol was involved."

The flying cycle required the KC-130 tankers to launch an hour prior to the fighters. The tanker was considerably slower and the additional time ensured the tanker would be on station, airborne checks complete, in a timely manner. The first tanker on track would have a short cycle. It had to top off the first fighters after their transit to the operations area and anytime they returned to the tanker. The fighters were scheduled to top off approximately every 45 minutes. This ensured a good fuel load at all times. More fuel would be required if visual identification runs (VID), some at supersonic speeds and high fuel consumption, were required. The first tanker topped off the second cycle of fighters when they arrived to leave the relief tanker with a full bag to give and itself with just enough fuel to return to Sakura. The relief tanker should have enough fuel give for the balance of night.

The relief tanker would have the longest cycle. In a perfect tanker rotation two tankers a night would suffice. To ensure there was always plenty of gas on station for the Hornet fighters the squadron rotated three tankers over a nine hour period. The last tanker was a short cycle and could be kept on deck by the second tanker if the second had plenty of gas remaining. A duty crew slept all night in the hangar in case the fourth or ready tanker had to launch. The Hornets had a similar cycle to ensure there was plenty of muscle on station and in reserve.

Crazy Calvin took the first turn and landed back at Sakura on schedule. Tumble had spoken to C2 in the maintenance control area earlier in the evening. C2 was sitting on a ragged overstuffed chair. His dog was on the deck next to the chair. The parachute cord leash was casually draped across C2's knees.

Crazy Cal had eyes that sparkled as if filled with dime store glitter. The right eye was a glacial blue and the left eye was walnut brown. His mouth was in a perpetual tight smile even if he was angry. It was as if he had once taken everything seriously and now took nothing seriously. No one knew if C2 was really crazy. Wild Bill handled him gingerly.

C2 had broken service. He had left the active duty Marine Corps for five years. That fact was in his squadron personnel record. He was rumored to have believed all and risked all flying in Africa and South America fighting communist, or terrorist, or the enemy de jour for his employer. He believed in the fight against evil doctrines and evil people and neither revisionist history nor time could change his mind. The little wars smoldered low and he returned to the active duty Marine Corps. There, he would languish, another old major, waiting on twenty years service because even knights errant wake up and realize they will need a pension and a medical plan. He had missed too many Xs to be promoted. He had spent all of his time in combat or flying tours, no staff tours to round him out, no colonels endorsing his fitness reports.

Still, some of his actions were exceedingly strange. There was his dog which was not a dog. It was an empty, red steel, coffee can with a nail hole driven through the rim. Through the hole was tied a length of dirty white parachute cord. The cord was used as a leash. When C2 went to fly he would hand the leash to the enlisted plane captain with instructions to have the dog, Folger, waiting for him when he landed.

Folger was a fixture for the young squadron marines. They recognized the XO, C2, as a leader and the mystery and rumor of his career enthralled them.

Wild Bill had tried to enforce a no pets rule. It made him look foolish when he applied it to an empty coffee can. Rule enforcement applied to a can meant he would have to admit his squadron executive officer had a can on a string and called the can a dog and named it.

C2 did not care that he was a major without hope of promotion. He wanted to continue doing the best flying he could find. Wild Bill had tried to shuffle him away but a Silver Star and two Distinguished Flying Crosses, all with classified citations, made him untouchable as long as he stayed reasonably felony free. Occasionally, his gyro tumbled but Wild Bill knew C2 was an old friend of the wing Commanding General and he did not want to go there. Though crazy, C2 was a capable officer and a good pilot and the marines loved him. He would retire soon.

Tumble liked to arrive early at his airplane. It helped him shift to flying gear, gave him time to compartmentalize, push extraneous thoughts to the back of his mind. He wanted the sense of aircraft and flight, the odor of jet fuel and lubricants, and the touch of aluminum.

He liked to enter the cockpit and look around while it was cold. It was like peering into a lair. The odors were peculiar to a cockpit. The Marine Hercs had decades of continuous military aviation behind them. The large Herc cockpit area was a utilitarian space and engendered a certain confidence. Tumble checked his watch. They were scheduled to be in the air by 0330, on station by 0415.

The first flight Tumble could remember had been a flight on a cold night like this one. He had been five or six years old and his sister a year younger. His father, a crop duster pilot, had placed Tumble and his sister in the front seat of a 7AC Aeronca Champ. It was Christmas time and they were very young and Christmas was exciting. Tumble remembered his father's smile as he put the one seat belt across both of them. He remembered the scent of brown, cracked leather seats, the engine and propeller noise and the initial fear. His sister was enthralled with the experience.

Overhead the small south Georgia town of Moultrie he had looked down on the courthouse square. The red, blue, green, and yellow Christmas lights crisscrossed the town streets like flowing stream borne colored bubbles. The colored lights came from the side streets and met at the courthouse square. The primary colored lights were orderly arranged and strung to the peak of the courthouse dome. There, on the silver dome, was a single, large, bright yellow star. The whole formed a beautiful Christmas tree appearance and all the while Tumble had been aware of the engine noise and the propeller noise of the small airplane. He had been cold and shivering, physically miserable. Tumble, after that flight, had known that the path to adventure was in an airplane for there; there everything was different, and changing, interesting, and exciting. Now, when Tumble entered an airplane cockpit alone and cold the thoughts of that childhood flight reflected back to him like sunlight from a mirror.

The Herc takeoff was a heavy, combat weight of 175,000 pounds and uneventful. Tumble complied with the most economical power settings and climb schedule airspeeds. They leveled at 23,000 feet and proceeded to the aerial refueling track. The tanker they would relieve was on track at 22,000 feet. Bongo checked in with the Navy Aegis cruiser monitoring all surface and air traffic and the Air Force aircraft, the Airborne Warning and Control System or AWACS, controlling all airborne aircraft. The relieved tanker called clear at the exit point and the AWACS descended Tumble to 22,000 feet.

Monotony took over. They monitored the radios but little concerned them. Hornets came, gassed, and left.

The sun was breaking the horizon as an electric pink ribbon when two Hornets came for the last planned refueling. Bongo was working the radios and doing paper work to keep track of which fighter squadron was to pay for the gas. The Hornets had just been cleared to plug when the AWACS called with bogies inbound. The Hornets disengaged from the tanker without taking fuel and were vectored toward the Korean peninsula.

The alert sounded short notice, unusual. Often Russian long range reconnaissance aircraft came down from Vladivostok. There was a lot of notice when the big Bears came. This kept the tension a few notches lower without losing intelligence and let the watchers know they were watched. The AWACS, the U.S. Air Force airborne aircraft with exceptional capabilities, was able to monitor the takeoffs and watch the Russian aircraft head south. No surprises made for a safer game. This early detection gave lead time, ensured the fighters were topped off, and positioned to intercept and escort the Russian recce aircraft by the fleet. It was a precaution. All Russian long range recce aircraft had bomber counterparts. No one expected a real problem with the Russians. It was a different nation from the days of the Soviet Empire but it was still an aggressive, strong, proud, and sovereign nation. The Russians wanted the U.S. Navy to know it was watched and the Navy provided a fighter escort to let the Russians know that the Navy was prepared anytime. A formalized game as long as it was in hand. The Russian and Navy aircrews had standing sight gags with one another ranging from centerfolds to high end Russian vodka bottles.

The pucker factor increased if the aircraft headed toward the fleet were from the northern part of the Korean Peninsula, the DPRK, the Democratic People's Republic of Korea. Everyone knew, or thought they knew, that the North Koreans were volatile. Since the Korean truce of 1953 there had been a stream of deadly incidents involving North Korean aggression. Their historic relationship with their neighbors and the Americans was one of sporadic and dangerous aggressiveness. The North Korean military had attacked and killed 2 American Army officers in the demilitarized zone and wounded several Republic of Korea service members when the U.S. Army led unarmed group had gone to cut a view obstructing tree. The North Koreans had lured aircraft into their territory with false navigation signals, a process known as meaconing, and, by such methods, had captured aircraft and crews. There was concern the DPRK might try to relive its glory day. That day the North Koreans had attacked an American intelligence gathering ship, the USS Pueblo, in international waters killing 2, capturing 82 American sailors and making the USS Pueblo a museum piece. The actual attack on the USS Pueblo had been preceded by the over flight of two MiG-21s. The Israeli Air Force had made a similar attack on the USS Liberty killing 34 and wounding 171 but, at least, the Israeli government had said they were sorry and had come up with a plausible story which the American government chose to accept.

The approaching bandits had been observed taking off from a coastal North Korean airfield. The AWACS had watched the formation join up, the sudden turn east, and the sprint toward the Sea of Japan, the East Sea, and the U.S. Navy fleet. The North Koreans had never attacked a fleet exercise but, like a bad dog that barks and sometimes bites, they wanted to make a barking rush. Maybe the Americans would do something stupid. The North Koreans thought their act earned respect.

The North Koreans had some older Russian built Beagle reconnaissance aircraft but those would normally be flown single ship. Dual bandits were headed seaward and that meant fighters, MiGs or Chinese copies of MiGs.

The Marine Hornets formed up for a high speed visual identification pass. The wingman, at supersonic speed, would be the looker and the lead the shooter. The Hornet wanted to make the VID before the bandits crossed the picket duty destroyer.

Tumble watched the startling blue, red, and, yellow comet from the dual engine nozzles as the looker Hornet went to afterburner and gobbled fuel as it headed west, at supersonic speed, into the still dark sky. The MiGs would see a fleet carrier with the rising sun behind it. The Hornet radar would pick up the visitors but a visual at the nautical sunrise would be a challenge. The delicate question of whether or not the shooter would have to shoot required all the information obtainable and a big balls decision.

Bongo acknowledged the AWACS vector turning the Herc to follow the fighters, close the gap for them if they needed a quick drink. They monitored the disembodied voices between the fighters and the AWACS as the later vectored the former. It was normally a game of escort and watch but the situation had to be approached like the rendezvous at the OK Corral.

"See 'em," said the looker.

"Yeah," prodded the shooter.

"Two MiG-21s. Atolls and drop tanks. They're just coming out to play," said the looker.

"All GCA guidance and no active MiG radar. Escort them," said the AWACS controller.

"Join on me. What's your gas?" said the shooter to the looker.

Tumble knew the supersonic looker would be lower on fuel than the shooter and that the Hornets would reform in a combat spread to escort the MiG-21s. Atolls were Soviet designed, heat seeking, air-to-air missiles and drops were extra fuel tanks. The good news was the MiGs were not armed with anti-shipping missiles or bombs. The bad news was that they were a threat to aircraft and the closest easy target was the Herc.

"The MiGs are going low," said Hornet lead.

The VID pass was over and the MiGs were dropping down to deck level to make a pass by the fleet without expecting to be shot. The American Hornets would accompany them. The MiG drop tank indicated a two way flight and not a Kamikaze attack planned. They wanted to see and be seen. The armament was self protection. The North Korean pilots had seen the cowboy movies.

The fighter lead continued his laconic commentary. It confirmed what the AWACS could see on radar.

The rising sun silhouetted the aircraft carrier Bobby Lee. The MiGs maneuvered in a wide ranging arc to line up for a parallel pass, a move calculated to not be confused with a weapons run.

The AWACS turned the Herc back toward the Bobby Lee and the now descending Hornets. The looker had used a lot of fuel during the supersonic run and would want to refuel soon. Tumble did not see the four low flying fighters or the carrier. He saw the small wake of an escort and a ship dot.

"Gotta go. Need gas," said the Hornet wingman.

The AWACS detached the wingman and kept the lead trailing the MiGs.

"Observers up," said Rodeo in the Herc cockpit.

"Hoses out as soon as you are ready," said Tumble.

The thirsty Hornet placed the probe in the refueling basket on the first attempt. It guzzled a long drink and left to rejoin the lead.

The sunrise was in full glory and the MiGs took the circuitous, scenic view and looked over the number and disposition of the ships in the carrier task force. The MiG-21s had to be sucking fuel fumes themselves but the pilots were afraid to go home until they had completed their mission.

The wingman bustered back to relieve the lead.

Tumble heard the lead Hornet request a turn with the tanker. The AWACS sent him toward the Herc.

"Looks like they have seen enough," said the Hornet wingman.

"They are climbing and turning toward the house. New bandits outbound," said the AWACS controller.

"How much gas, Rodeo?" said Tumble.

Tumble knew the alert pad Hornets would be launched for the new bandits. Every bad guy needed an escort. The Hornets would buster at near supersonic speed, too and would want a top off at the first opportunity.

Rodeo gave Tumble the fuel state. They were due to go off station soon but the situation was changing fast.

"Bongo, call on squadron common and have the ready tanker manned. We won't be going home on time. If the North Koreans keep relaying MiGs out here the sky will be full of jets and ours will need all the fuel they can get. Make sure the AWACKY knows," said Tumble.

Five minutes later the AWACS launched the ready Herc tanker. Another crew was called in to man a cold tanker. The second set of MiGs flew a non-aggressive recon path. The alert Hornets would run a fuel consuming high speed visual ID with a shooter in position.

The Navy had learned hard lessons, in the Persian Gulf, a few years prior to the First Gulf War when a pilot of Saddam Hussein's Iraq Air Force flying a Mirage F1 ignored verbal challenges and fired two French manufactured Exocet anti-ship missiles at the guided missile frigate USS Stark. The hits had killed thirty-seven American sailors and wounded twenty-one. The Navy returned to a stand your ground concept of self defense. A year later this led to the tragic, mistaken identity shoot down, by the USS Vincennes, of a civilian airliner killing all 290 people aboard Iran Air Flight 655. Technology wasn't everything it was advertised to be. Therefore, it was often good to put human eyeballs on potential targets.

The Marines prepared another set of land based Hornets for launch. Aboard the Bobby Lee the schedule changed and the time for the first launch of the day was moved up. The carrier had squadrons of single seat F/A-18E Super Hornets and two seat F/A-18F Super Hornets. The single-seaters were primarily for air to air fighting but were very capable of ground attack. The two-seaters were primarily configured for surface attacks but were capable of air to air combat.

The North Koreans wanted to break the rhythm of the U.S. fighter cycle, overload the Navy's ability to keep up the intercepts and embarrass the Navy and the United States government for coming into waters the North Koreans claimed as territorial waters. The North Koreans had hundreds of fighters within range of the coast. The fighters were mostly older Russian built MiG models or Chinese copies of various capability and maintainability in their inventory. The single Navy carrier and the land based Marines had about a hundred primary fighters. Ordinarily there would be two to six fighters airborne. There were other tactical aircraft that could be called on to help escort the North Koreans. This was not the preferred course and neither was being forced from international waters. The situation was shaping up to be a goat roping contest.

Tumble and crew had given away all the fuel they could. They could no longer make the trip back to Sakura. They declared a fuel emergency and landed at the Republic of Korea air base at Pohang. They refueled and coordinated a launch back into the exercise area. Now there were two tanker Hercs and the AWACS sent them to stations at opposite ends of the area. A Russian Tupelov TU-142 Bear long range reconnaissance aircraft was on the way down from the north for party time. The Navy requested the Hercs stay on station for their fighters. The Navy wanted to hold their fast buddy tanker Hornets on deck to fill gaps.

It was after 1200 before Tumble and his crew returned to base. They had expected to be back by 0800. During the day the pace slackened but every ninety minutes the North Koreans sent out another pair of MiGs, sometimes 21s and sometimes 23s. Occasionally, the MiGs turned back at intercept and occasionally they continued. The MiGs maneuvered slowly, never making any moves that could be considered preparation for a weapons run. The Navy kept the interceptions coming.

Night two and the Marine tanker schedule was the same though all expected to go long and all Hercs were prepared for launch. The challenge from the North Koreans had put excitement in the air.

Night three, the unrelenting tempo was no longer exciting. It was drudgery. The crews were determined they would not be driven from the skies. The North Koreans, with a little help from their long range Russian friends, continued their steady launch pattern. The tempo required the Navy to be prepared to launch during their maintenance and rest period. It wasn't that they could not do twenty-four hour cycles, extend ex, it was that a little help was appreciated, made things easier. The North Koreans increased the tempo in the pre dawn, the balance of night when the body's Circadian rhythm was at a low point. Using their ground based radar to watch the American fighters the North Koreans could tell how long each crew had been on station and who should be tired, nearing the end of their night shift. The North Koreans would like to embarrass the Americans, drive the Americans from the East Sea of Korea operations area short of the advertised week of operations. It would be their victory.

Day four a weather front began to push through with rain, rime icing, and low ceilings. The cloud tops were in the mid twenties. Every launch and recovery was instrument flying. The North Korean MiGs had minimal anti-icing and limited instrument landing capability. The Air Force of the Democratic People's Republic of Korea changed to the Russian built Ilyushin IL-28 Beagle. The Il-28 was a capable vintage Soviet design mid-range bomber with a bomb bay to hide weaponry from prying eyes. The North Koreans launched individual Beagles twenty minutes apart, gave them overlapping cycles, and flew them over the fleet at altitude. The sea surface was not visible to the Beagle crews but the aircraft loiter time was considerably greater than the MiGs. As long as a Beagle was on station it required an escort.

The Navy instantly recognized the problem. There would be no short breaks as with the MiG cycles. The Navy increased the number of fighters in their CAPS. The Beagle technique was to cross the coast line and stay in the cloud tops. When their RHAW (radar homing and warning) gear indicated American fighter radar they would pop through the top of the clouds. The Beagles had to be met as they crossed into international waters. Radar intercepts with altitude separation were needed and as soon as the Beagle broke out on top the Navy wanted a Hornet to be the first thing the Beagle crew saw. A decision would be required if a Beagle cycled bomb bay doors open. The North Korean ground controllers had thought this out. They limited the times for the VIDs and told their aircraft when to duck back into the clouds, turn back toward the mainland and then reverse course back toward the fleet. The same Beagle, in and out, could require multiple intercepts. A couple of Navy Hornets went to in close weather formation flying scant feet off each wing of the Beagle, but higher powers decided it was too provocative and pulled the Hornets back to use their radar to shadow the DPRK Beagles.

Hornets with buddy stores for air refueling found themselves being vectored for intercepts. The Herc Marines brought up more flight crews from Okinawa and went to port and starboard duty watches. The fuel load was increased to war weights for all the KC-130 tankers. Flying was day and night. The sky was crowded.

The North Koreans added a new wrinkle. They possessed far fewer IL-28s than MiGs. They sent their patrol boats to sea.

The patrol boats, some known to carry anti-ship armament either missiles or torpedoes, stayed fifty miles from the nearest American ship, still within missile range. They made large circuits and then, from the back side of the circuit, would rush across the sea to their self imposed fifty mile limit and then turn back. The patrol boats required continual monitoring with surface search radar. The Navy moved their destroyers to an intimidating distance, also a vulnerable distance.

Night five was a reunion. Bongo recognized Dirt's voice as a Hornet came in for gas. The boys were on their shift.

Night six was more of the same. Night seven and endex, end of exercise, was scheduled for 0900 the following morning. Everyone was ready to finish. Tumble and crew had drawn the graveyard shift all the way through. Better to get in a sleep pattern and keep it than constantly change shifts. After the first busy day, the remainder of the Herc squadron joining them, the tankers had flown a staggered two ship and added another two ship launch to their cycle to support the Navy in the busy time before dawn. The North Koreans had figured out the change over from the Marine Sakura based fighters and the carrier fighters. The additional morning Herc shift supplied the jet fuel, the JP. The Navy put a couple of pure fighters in the air and left the buddy store configured fighters for spot support.

Tumble walked to the back of the aircraft relieved himself, talked to the crew members, slapped shoulders, and offered low key compliments. He had a good crew and they had responded in an excellent manner. The enlisted crewmembers flew missions and helped maintain the aircraft. They had put in long hours averaging fifteen duty hours with a couple of make it happen days at eighteen plus hours.

Don Juan was ever present around the flight line and hangar before the Herc launches. He brought the fighter group Chaplain, Navy Captain O'Grady, with him a couple of times. The Chaplain moved between the fighter squadrons and the orphan tanker squadron. He had an impromptu standup comedy routine that was a tension reliever for whatever group of marines he was with. The jokes were old and stale but appreciated. He made himself available for quiet talks. The Chaplain had been an enlisted marine, an M-60 machine gunner, in the First Gulf War and still carried a hard nose reputation the enlisted marines appreciated.

Don Juan talked to everyone, gauging the health and fatigue of the air crews and maintenance crews. He watched them as they listened to the

Chaplain's jokes. Chaplain O'Grady understood no one wanted bullshit. All understood a lost crew would be a defeat.

Tumble had found himself flying, running, eating, sleeping; flying, running, eating, sleeping. He was tired but thought he had another day or two left in him. He knew it was harder on the enlisted marines, the fighter crews, the sailors who were launching and recovering aircraft eighteen hours a day. The aircraft maintenance ashore and afloat required thirty hours stuffed into a twenty-four hour day. The skies were watched around the clock by shore and ship based radar and the ever airborne Air Force AWACS crews out of Okinawa.

The weather improved night last and the North Koreans surged their launch cycle to a pair every forty-five minutes. They launched MiG-21s, and 23s, and 29s and threw the Beagles in high. The Russians came down and sat in the upper bleachers. The North Koreans had sensed or knew this was the last night of the exercise and upped their pressure. The sky was a traffic jam.

The AWACS ran the intercepts and the Aegis cruiser became the air traffic controller ensuring altitude and horizontal separation for the Hornets cycling in and out of the area and kept track of the DPRK patrol boats as they rushed an invisible line and turned back before the Navy took aggressive defensive measures. They had to be watched because there was no guarantee they would always turn back. A North Korean submarine had torpedoed a Republic of Korea Naval vessel, the

Cheonan, and killed forty-six sailors in recent times. In addition to watching the North Korean Air Force and the patrol boats the Navy had a full time submarine screen in action. It was training and almost not as it was close to the real thing. It was the type of training money could not buy and all hoped it stayed in the training category.

Rent notified Tumble they were at their max distance from a divert field since the start of the exercise. The bingo into Pohang on day one had been embarrassing as that was not the designated divert.

Tumble checked Bongo and wondered if he looked as worn as Bongo. His eyeballs had that sanded with a fine grit sandpaper feeling. He could smell his own body odor wafting up from his fire retardant Nomex flight suit. The choice was sleep or wash clothes and even with two flight suits for a week the unwashed scent was making a statement. He had set a personal best for the number of cups of bad coffee in a week. All in all it was a great day to be a United States Marine. A demanding mission had been successfully executed. Marines, and sailors, and airmen and their equipment had functioned as advertised, mostly. Tumble had not given a thought to his personal problems or life since the operational tempo had increased. Wild Bill had not even bothered to bring up the horse back dancing episode and while his multiple sprained fingers had kept him from piloting a Herc he had launched with a different crew each day. Wild Bill had not flown with Tumble's crew which was fine with all concerned.

Tumble yawned and asked for more of the bad, black, coffee. He checked his Rolex GMT, a wedding present. He had not heard an alert for another two-ship of North Korean MiGs coming out to play. Maybe they had quit. The section of tankers he had replaced had done only normal tanking evolutions and the Hornets had not flown any intercepts. In the east Tumble saw, above the black velvet band of the earth's shadow, the almost unreal hues of red and purple and gold in the eastern sky, the precursor of day.

The bad coffee was better than no coffee. He saw Bongo's chin had dropped to his chest. A pool of snuff drool was on his flight suit. He glanced over his right shoulder and saw Rodeo had locked his shoulder harness and was sitting straight up. The dropped chin and wet spot of drool on his chest said he was asleep. They had earned their stolen moment. Rodeo had worked through the day helping to ready his Herc and the others for the final night push.

Gunner Rent was standing. He held up two fingers and pointed to Tumble and himself and then smiled. He was monitoring the radios and their position and ensuring at least two were awake on the flight deck.

Tumble spoke to the loadmaster and observer, in the back, by intercom. The loadmaster a thirty plus year master gunnery sergeant answered immediately. Tumble figured the Top, at the left observer position, was smoking to stay awake. The Herc always had a draft around the aft cargo door and ramp that sucked the smoke out. Sometimes the gap was so big they had pressurization issues and stuffed damp rags into the gaps.

The young lance corporal answered from the right observation position. The position was at the right paratroop door and it had a window in it. The master guns would be able to see the lance corporal and that would be enough to keep him awake.

The windows in the two paratroop doors, one behind each wing, were aligned such that the observers could watch the receiver aircraft as they plugged for fuel. The observers provided indispensible observation and commentary for the safety of the refueling evolution. In the event of a mid-air collision ejection seats gave the receiver aircraft a last chance. The Herc carried parachutes but no one wore them. The location of the huge 3,600 gallon internal fuselage fuel tank located along the longitudinal center axis of the fuselage allowed a narrow passage for the crewmembers, too narrow for passage while wearing a parachute and the only feasible parachute exits were aft of the fuselage fuel tank which was also aft of the propellers. No one forward bothered to wear a parachute and aft the crew normally declined in deference to the front end crew or because the parachutes restricted movement past the tank. No one expected to have time to use a parachute if there was a mid-air collision.

Tumble stood beside his seat, wearing his headset, and stretched. He noticed a change in the voice of the AWACS controller before he understood the call. Bandits were launching and it was kickoff time. He heard the vectors for the fighters. Several minutes later another MiG section was spotted coming out.

The first set of bandits neared the outer ring of ship self contained defense and turned to fly parallel to the course of the task force thereby drawing their Hornet escorts away from the air corridor the MiGs had used all week. The bandits then turned toward the known location of a North Korean air base that had not been used during the exercise. The AWACS gave a vector for an intercept of a second set of bogies.

There was one section of two Marine Hornets airborne. No one was available to escort the two retreating MiGs all the way to their new exit point. They would be low fuel and going home.

The Hornets turned away from the departing MiGs and toward the arriving pair. The Hornets went to burner and accelerated supersonic to make a timely intercept.

Below, ship klaxons blared to wake the dead and the sleeping and the 1MC voice called, "general quarters, general quarters. All hands man your battle stations." The Navy was going to a task force wide general quarters. Sailors, more asleep than awake, rolled from their racks and surged to their appointed stations, securing water tight hatches behind them and readying themselves for their individual and collective responsibilities.

The AWACS controllers recognized the beginning of a surge and called back to MCAS Sakura to launch the ground alert fighters. Every MiG flight had to be intercepted, no free passes.

The two Hornets on intercept called their fuel states. The AWACS checked the figures, left one Hornet with the MiGs and vectored the lower fuel state Hornet toward a rendezvous point and called the Herc out of the holding pattern to meet the Hornet. Tumble knew the alert Hornets would buster out at a prodigious fuel consumption rate and require fuel, the fuel he carried, soon after arriving. He had Bongo coordinate the launch of the standby Herc tanker as it would take forty-five minutes to arrive in the area. Tumble knew his fuel give would increase geometrically, the number of Hornets was doubling and the use of afterburner would increase the give requirement even further.

The number of days in the exercise was public knowledge, in theory, that was to help keep a lid on incidents. The exact endex time was not published knowledge. Now, the North Koreans were holding their own exercise. They were actively jamming radar for the first time and attempting to overwhelm the Navy's ability to intercept each probing sortie. They would like nothing more than to break through the air defense ring unescorted. Get a photo of one of their jets in an unescorted flyby of an American ship or force the Americans to withdraw prior to endex or end of exercise time. It would be embarrassing and humiliating for the American Navy and a great victory for them. It was a game of chicken.

Below, the Navy task force commander issued orders to early launch the carrier borne fighter CAP. Sailors had worked through the night readying their jets for a scheduled 0600 launch. The Hornets were ready to go but there are details that have to be accomplished just prior to launch. The sailors turned to, skill and drill guiding fatigued bodies and minds. Navy chiefs were everywhere among the young sailors checking, observing, and correcting. The chiefs knew what they always know that there is danger in rushed performance which is not the same as quick and smooth. Do the task the same way every time, no short cuts. If something does not feel right then something is wrong. The flight deck of an operating carrier carries a high degree of exposure to deadly danger during the most routine operations. Season the launch and recovery with urgency and the potential dangers for sailors and aircrew are increased. The chiefs know that the officers have a hierarchal responsibility as there is always the need to have someone to hang in the spirit of Voltaire and Admiral Byng, "pour encourager les autres." However, it is the Navy chiefs who make the job happen correctly.

The two-seat Hornet on the number one bow catapult was manned by Dirt and Spider. Spider was finishing his honey bun from the dirty shirt ward room and wanting a cup of coffee as the plane captain reached down to fasten the Koch fittings of his body harness to the ejection seat and parachute system. Spider had to lean forward and connect his leg gaiters and in so doing dropped his honey bun to the bottom of the cockpit. He gave the sailor's obligatory curse. Dirt signaled, from the back seat, that he was ready and Spider gave up the honey bun recovery.

The launch officer signaled Spider. The catapult crew and final checkers swarmed the jet. Feeling the need of a shave and a chance to pee he looked at the wingman and saw a thumbs up. He checked the canopy closed and set the throttles. The catapult officer twirled his fingers and kicked for burner. Spider lit the afterburner and saluted. Dirt had been braced to go for the past fifteen seconds.

The Hornet accelerated from zero past 150 knots in two and a half heart beats and the Hornet was airborne off the cat stroke. Spider retracted the gear and flaps, his wingman signaled aboard, and the pair of Hornets accelerated toward the intercept area as Dirt checked in with the AWACS. Behind them the next set of Hornets was in position to launch, on demand, from the waist catapults and two more Hornets were guided onto the recently vacated bow cats.

"What do you think, Dirt?" Spider asked as they completed their climb and systems checks.

"The bad guys are trying to juke us, partner. We have to be ready for this to turn nasty. Play it cool but be ready to shoot."

"There are a lot of jets up here. We'll need the VIDs."

The North Korean MiG-21s or the Chinese twin the F-7 and MiG-23s continued to launch every fifteen minutes. Multiple sections of North

Korean fighters were always airborne and they were mixing their launch and recovery air bases to maximize the intercept and escort distances required of the Hornets. The AWACS went with the flow and directed the Hornets returning from the far point to meet the escorts instead of going all the way back to the intercept points. Soon, the Marine and Navy Hornets had two big coordinated loops, right hand rotation with a thousand feet of vertical separation in the hand off to be adjusted as required. The MiGs were unescorted for a few minutes but they were away from surface ships and, by then, had been checked for anti-ship missiles.

The North Koreans were smart. They expected adaptation on the part of the American Navy. A dozen MiGs were now at their southern air base. They were refueled and launched back out, moving an intercept point to the south and still launching from a northern airbase. Two additional sections of Marine Hornets were already on the way and would be able to make intercepts on the MiGs out from the southern launch base. Three more Herc tankers were enroute and another pair was being manned for launch. Below all the USS Bobby Lee readied additional fighters but held them on the cats.

Tumble checked his fuel and position. He bounced his figures off Bongo, Rodeo, and Rent. He figured they could give away another 12,000 pounds of JP, jet fuel, and stay on station another half an hour and the relief tankers would arrive as they reached bingo fuel. If they gave more they would have to leave sooner or go to the divert base.

Give away more fuel and leave sooner or less and stay longer. He wondered if the Navy was tracking the give fuel and launching buddy store Hornets that could escort MiGs or provide get home fuel to other Hornets. He had enough concerns without chasing a rabbit that was not his. This was a play it to make it situation.

The North Koreans brought out one more trick. They began coordinated launches from their northern and southern coastal air bases with Mig-21s, -23s, 29s and IL-28s from interior bases. A second Russian Bear would arrive soon from Vladivostok. The zone was flooded.

The AWACS and ship radars saw multiple launches from multiple air bases. It was a surprise in that few thought the North Koreans could coordinate such an effort. The Bobby Lee launched the ready fighters and rolled more onto the catapults. The Marines launched more Hornets from Sakura across the Sea of Japan, the East Sea, and the last of the war weighted Herc tankers strained their way into the air. One tanker went solo and set up a holding pattern half way between Sakura and the exercise area to provide emergency refueling for homeward bound Marine Hornets or wayward Navy fighters.

The Navy launched an E-2 Hawkeye, a small carrier borne AWACS type aircraft, to take an assigned load from the big four-engine Air Force E-3 Sentry AWACS. The Aegis cruiser monitored the airborne developments and tracked the milling

North Korean patrol boats now numbering two dozen.

Now, the dawn was in Marine colors of scarlet and gold. Tumble could see a sky full of jets sparkling in the morning sunlight. His trained eye instantly recognized the silhouettes of one and two-seat Hornets, MiG-21s and -23s, and 29s.

A single Hornet came to them and took a quick 4,000 pounds before rushing back to the intercept area.

The AWACS began to break up sections and send Hornets on single ship intercepts. Tumble knew the fighter bubbas would not like that but until more cavalry arrived it was the temporary solution to no unescorted MiGs on a fleet flyby. He called for another fuel and position check. The Herc crew had been very busy for some time now. No extraneous chatter, all business. He could sense the tenseness, and fatigue, but he also sensed the pride coming from the crew.

"Rover 22, Rover 22,"said the AWACS controller. There was a voice inflection change from previous calls. "Rover you have two bandits approaching from your four o'clock. Make an immediate turn to zero four zero."

Bongo acknowledged. It was their call sign. Tumble complied bringing the Herc around and calling for a fuel check. The heading would turn them further away from a Sakura recovery.

"We can make Misawa, if we have to," Rent said.

Tumble acknowledged. Rent was ahead of the game. Misawa had U.S. Air Force fighters and Navy patrol elements based there, the northern part of Honshu Island.

The AWACS turned a solo Hornet toward them in an effort to cut off the bandits. In their repositioning for quicker accessibility to the fighters the Herc was positioned underneath the Hornet escort swap over point. Not the ideal tanker anchor but since there was no shooting it was a better location for the Hornets. The location had put them closer to the MiGs and the North Korean controllers had taken notice. Now, the North Korean attitude was max intimidation of all the Americans, not some of the Americans.

"If you're not a fighter you're a target," Tumble said. It was an old O Club bar taunt and had started more than one fight. That did not make it any less true.

"Hey, hey Texaco," a voice said on the refueling frequency. "Got you on radar. Got two MiGs closing from your six. We're buster."

"Sounds like Dirt," said Bongo. It was his first nonessential comment in an hour.

"I think you're right," said Tumble.

"Come on, Dirt. You guys owe us," Bongo transmitted.

"What do you know? Bongo the hose dragger?"

"That's us."

"We're burner and solo. Our companero already has company."

"You are welcome."

"Rover 22, bandits are closing, ten miles, six o'clock, your altitude. That thing got anymore speed?" said the AWACS controller.

The MiG-21s went to afterburner accelerating and adjusting their altitude to a few feet below the Herc. They blew by underneath each wing of the Herc and pulled up sharply in front of it. The force of the displaced air thumped the Herc and violently jostled it. The MiGs rolled right and left.

Tumble over controlled to correct and added to the oscillations. He recognized the error, reduced power and went light on the controls and let the Herc stabilize itself wings level, slight descent. He added power, trimmed, and leveled at the original altitude.

The MiG-21s came out of afterburner and arched back around for the rejoin and maneuvering toward the six of the Herc. They did not see the single Hornet and it was lost to the North Korean Ground Control Intercept radar in a sky full of jets.

"Sir, I got 'em, two of 'em, coming back around. Turning toward us and coming in from 4 o'clock," said the young lance corporal at the starboard paratroop door observer position.

"Tell AWACky we are out of 220," said Tumble. He heard Bongo make the call. He kept the power up and nosed over pushing the light weight Herc past the normal limiting airspeed. He figured the Lockheed boys had a few knots of slop for mama. The extra speed would not be much to the MiGs but he wanted the Hornet on scene and visible when the MiGs caught him again. He thought about a turn into the MiG to throw off their shoot solution. He decided he was not at that point. Hornet help would be appreciated.

"Visual, we got a visual," transmitted Dirt on the AWACS frequency.

"Roger, visual. We show the MiGs rejoining; maneuvering back to the tanker six. Confirm."

"Affirmative; request nose hot."

"Standby on nose hot."

"Think those MiGs know we're here, Spider?"

"Let's show them, Dirt."

Spider maneuvered into the MiG six and went to afterburner.

The MiGs slowed their closure rate and pulled into position behind the Herc. The Herc crew could not see them but the MiG pilots knew the AWACS could see the maneuvers.

Spider drove his Hornet scant feet below the lead MiG-21 and then pulled into the vertical in front of the lead, behind and just outside the Herc's starboard wing. He closed out the burner and rolled right as he topped the adjunct formation of MiGs and Herc.

The MiG was matching the Herc speed and the shock wave thumped against the smaller MiG and tossed it about in twisting and uncoordinated flight. The Herc trembled and bobbled left but Tumble was ready for this, his second thump in five minutes. The flight control problem was the same whether it was a good guy or a bad guy who administered the thump.

"Hello, asshole," transmitted Dirt not really caring if the MiG pilots could hear him. It would give the Herc bubbas comfort.

The lead MiG pilot regained control but did not react to the Hornet lure. It was, most likely, a possible scenario the MiG pilots had briefed. The MiG lead maneuvered back behind the Herc and stabilized there to show he was not intimidated. He had not been prepared to turn onto the Hornet tail. Spider had counted on that, the surprise of the maneuver, to get him past a dicey spot.

"They know we are here," Spider said to Dirt. He wrapped the Hornet around in a tight decelerating turn and maneuvered behind the MiGs.

"These guys don't scare easy," said Dirt.

"MiGs or the Herc?" said Spider.

"Can't tell from here about the Herc boys but I see the MiGs going about their assigned duties."

"I'm going to pull forward just enough to give the MiGs a peek. Let them know we are back here. Let 'em see the Sidewinders; then drop back out of sight behind them."

"We wouldn't use Sidewinders back here? Those heat seekers would fly up the Herc exhaust; take it down."

"That won't be a worry. If we shoot it will be a revenge killing, not Herc help."

"Bird Dog, what is the scoop on weapons hot?" Dirt transmitted to the AWACS.

"Standby on weapons hot," was the reply.

"Tumble, slow it down and make the MiGs undershoot," Dirt transmitted. He had used Tumble's personal call sign. He knew that would increase the chance of the odd instruction penetrating the thoughts swirling through Tumble's mind.

Tumble maintained course. He did not want to overly surprise the MiGs and get rammed but he did not like them setting up a shooting range with his Herc as the target. He pulled all four throttles to flight idle and the gear horn sounded and red gear warning lights flashed. He maintained level flight with the nose just above the horizon. The airspeed fell away like water through a big mesh sieve.

The MiGs took immediate evasive action. The overtake rate surprised them. They were unsure if the Herc would maintain altitude. They throttled back, went nose low and wing over separating left and right. They were good.

Spider, expecting the maneuver had slowed and dropped back. He had the plummeting MiGs in sight.

"I got the lead, low on the right. You eyeball dash two," said Spider.

Tumble heard the observers call the MiGs and the Hornet in sight as the Herc hit approach to stall buffet and the wings trembled. Tumble pushed the throttles up. Mr. Lockheed and staff came through. The Allison T-56 engines always turned at 100% rpm in flight and blown prop air covered 40 per cent of the wing area. The Hamilton Standard props quickly varied their pitch to absorb the energy available from the increased fuel flow and engine power. The new volume of airflow over the wings gave almost instantaneous stall recovery.

"The MiGs are on a rejoin and leaving the area," said the AWACS controller. "Two more are coming from the southern base. They are headed for the tanker, not the ships."

"We're scochi on go juice. Got any help coming our way?" said Dirt.

"Looking for spares now. There is a flash mob rushing the Bobby Lee."

"We're buying," said Bongo. "We'll bring you aboard for a drink as soon as we get the speed up and the hoses back out."

"How much you got to give, buddy?" said Dirt.

"Three if we go back to Sakura."

"We're a long way from Mr. Lee and we have new bad guys to chase."

"Standby."

"The MiGs will be here soon, Tumble. What do you think?" said Bongo.

"Rent, how much do we need to make Pohang?"

"We're are not suppose to do that; suppose to leave the south Koreans out of this," said Bongo.

"Pohang is closer than Misawa and Sakura is out of the question. Our rule makers are sitting on the ground in an air conditioned office and worried about a political incident. We've already got an incident and their answer is O.B.E.," said Tumble.

"We can give eight and still land at Pohang with four engines running," said Rent. "No go-arounds."

"Rodeo, give the Hornet the gas. Eight if he can take it. He'll need all he can get to get us out of the crack."

"Aye, aye," said Rodeo.

"SOP says overhead the field, clear day with no less than six-thousand pounds," said Bongo.

"Thanks, but there won't be an overhead the field if that Hornet isn't here to help us. Tell the AWACS the plan and request the Pohang weather."

"The AWACS says we are not to proceed to Pohang."

"We are not asking permission. We are telling them. Declare an emergency and request the Pohang weather."

Tumble looked over at Bongo as he spoke. Bongo looked back, gave a broad grin and spit tobacco juice into a foam cup. Tumble could smell the fresh, wet tobacco.

"We're ready," said Rodeo.

"Clear the boys aboard," said Tumble.

The Hornet plugged and sucked the fuel.

"They have the fuel," Rodeo said as he threw switches and closed valves.

"You have your gas," said Bongo.

"Roger and thanks. Back to work," said Dirt.

Spider dropped back from the refueling basket and picked up an intercept heading from the AWACS.

Rent gave Tumble an adjusted heading for the Republic of Korea air base at Pohang.

The AWACS relayed the Pohang weather and did not remind them of the restriction against the use. The weather was not good, not bad. It was junk of a thousand feet ceiling and rain restricting the visibility to two miles. It was the same bowl of rocks he had not even attempted to land at with the truck marines. A different day called for a different way.

The approach and landing were uneventful. They refueled the Herc. Tumble pulled a Velcro squadron patch off his flight suit and gave it to the fuel truck driver. They launched back toward the operating area and checked in with a full bag.

The Navy was controlling air and sailing outbound. They put Tumble's Herc in a just in case pattern. The Navy had exercised the right of free passage on the high seas. The North Koreans had vehemently contested and restated their excessive sovereignty claims. Their honor was satisfied.

It had been a near run thing for the Navy. They had considered asking for U.S. Air Force fighter help from Misawa Air Force Base. That would have really been embarrassing.

The freedom of passage exercise would be repeated in a few months. A good time was had by all.

Chapter Twelve   Run with the Horse Dancer

Tumble walked into the BOQ with Bongo. He was tired but still keyed up. He knew it would be a waste of time to try and sleep. Bongo declined the invitation for a run. Tumble decided to go alone; run the sea wall; go into a runner's trance for an hour, come back, cold morning beer, hot shower and choose between sleeping or eating; maybe drop by the O Club in the evening. It was not much of a plan but it was a plan.

He was slipping into his runner gear when the thought of his wife, ex-wife, ambushed him. He could not picture her face. He dug into the bottom of his B-4 bag and pulled out a picture of her and their son. He had not looked at a photo in a long time. He was not sure why he did so now. He was very tired and his emotional guard was down. He felt tears well and he muttered a curse to stabilize himself. He was feeling sorry for himself. There, in the back corner of his heart and mostly hidden was what he failed to face or acknowledge. His son was no more. He no longer had a wife, a marriage, a family. He peeked at the thought and, not rejecting it, he simply forced it aside.

Outside a light morning mist was falling. The wind was down. It was not too cold. Shorts and sweat shirt were adequate for the run.

Tumble knew it would be a slow run. In the half mile it took him to reach the sea wall ramp he was running, smooth, easy, and had acknowledged to himself it would be a short run, maybe four miles.

He loved the scent of sea and the fine mist carried from it. The mist bore the life taste of the sea to his lips and from there to his tongue where he savored the salt, the faint fishiness, the rejuvenating effect. He imagined a briny crust forming on his brow. He loved it.

Faint and gentle he heard the steps of another runner overtaking him. He slowed a step to let the runner overtake and pass. He was not looking for company.

A new scent reached him. It rode atop the fragrance of the sea and was complimentary as a small and graceful boat on gentle swells. It was citrus atop gardenias and a pleasant muskiness. Feminine, teasing, alluring, and despite his fatigue held his attention, stirred him, an animal response to scent. Nothing to be proud of he joked mentally.

The runner approached from his left. He went into his politically correct and straight ahead stare. If the runner were a young, female, enlisted marine anything more than a nod could be a problem. Any young, male officer would go to great lengths to avoid even a moment alone with a young woman marine and rightly so if he had an iota of sense.

"Thought it was you," said a feminine voice.

Tumble looked. It was the horse dancer girl from happy hour, the one with the CO, Wild Bill. "Great," he thought, "wonderful."

"Hi," he said. His tone was neutral.

"Oh knock it off," she said. "I slapped you, the wrong guy. You bit me on the butt and we are even."

"It was not a slap."

"I learned to hit like that at home. I grew up with three brothers. Slap sounds more ladylike."

Tumble turned his head for a clearer look. She was short and athletically muscled. Her dark hair was pulled into a bobbed pony tail. Her eyes were green and gold flecked. Her stride was smooth and her breathing conditioned and easy. This was not her first run. Her arms showed biceps definition, maybe some weight lifting.

"Things got out of hand, sorry. I had one beer too many or maybe more than one too many."

"Me too; I don't really drink and it showed. Body weight ratio you know. Your CO is a witty guy and fun to be with."

Tumble glanced her way. She meant what she said. Wild Bill must have a special rapport with women that Tumble had not noticed. He did not comment and ran on in silence thinking she would move on.

"You are paranoid," she said. "I am trying to declare a truce."

"Ever hear of tail hook?"

"After last Friday I was wondering if you had."

"Ouch."

"Afraid to give me your name?"

"Tumble."

"Really, that is a name?"

"It's what I use."

"Jewel."

"Jewel?"

"What my mother named me, unlike yours."

"Okay."

"Okay."

"Are you going far?"

"Turn around where the sea wall stops."

"Sounds good; it has been a long week with the children. I'm an elementary teacher at the base school. This Department of Defense school teaching is a great job. I am here for two years and then to Europe."

They ran, mostly in silence, for another twenty minutes and curled back at the end of the sea wall for the return. Tumble found himself becoming comfortable in her presence. He visualized a yellow and black cross hatched danger sign.

They ran down the ramp from the sea wall and toward the visitor BOQ where Tumble was quartered. They had covered the where are you from and where did you go to college conversation. The routes split near the front gate. Jewel would go to the left toward the permanent party quarters.

As they approached the split Jewel gave Tumble an athletic pat on the shoulder. She laughed.

Tumble stopped in the road. He called after her, "how about a cup of coffee in town?" His next thought was, "how stupid are you?"

"Sure, thirty minutes. Meet you by the front gate."

She ran backwards a few steps, waved and turned around to run on to her quarters.

He stood in the road smiling. A Japanese taxi driver gave a polite horn reminder.

Shaved and showered and without sleep Tumble still felt great. He was familiar with Japanese coffee houses. They were expensive but relaxing. He ironed a pair of clean jeans and a faded yellow chamois shirt. He was warm and comfortable.

He arrived at the front gate on time. Ten minutes later Jewel arrived. Not bad for most of the women he knew. She wore fashionable skinny jeans, frilly white blouse and a stylish, short, light weight, leather jacket and tight, calf covering boots. She had just enough makeup on for highlights. Her pony tail was shaken out and her hair was slightly damp. She was pretty.

The mist was burning away with the morning and the sky was clearing.

Jewel slipped her arm in his and they walked through the front gate. Past the gate the world changed to shops catering to marines: tailor shops, bars, pawn shops, snack bars. They passed these and the further they walked the less they saw of English language signs in the shop windows. They turned toward town center and passed a Japanese cemetery with small obelisks and memorial markers crowded together. Not much of a grave plot is required for cremation remains.

Very personable one on one the Japanese tended to avoid eye contact in public groups. Tumble felt invisible as they walked in the shopping district. There were numberless bicycles parked in the ginza, the shopping area. He was curious about that. He saw lots and lots of cars on the road and relatively few bicycles yet upon arrival downtown he saw hundreds of bicycles parked together.

The scents were motivation enough for travel and an adventure just in the enjoyment of them, their difference and strangeness, and some could be tasted in the air. He could close his eyes and be magically moved about to exotic world corners and by sniffing the air he could tell in which country the wizard had settled him. The city scent of Japan was pleasant even near busy streets where diesel fumes from the trucks and propane exhaust from the taxis mingled with what Tumble found to be unusual foods, spices, and cooking methods. It was a mélange that called his soul to adventure.

They passed his favorite type of Japanese vending machine. In English signage was advertised soft drinks, canned coffees, and remon (sic) tea spelled out phonetically, if you were Japanese.

A second type of street side vending machine sold small bottles of Japanese whiskey. He had tried it and the whiskey had a unique taste that was okay if he did not try to classify it in an American whiskey category.

He took the time to point these things out to Jewel. She was in her first year overseas and a couple of years out of college. It was just enough age difference for Tumble to be conscious of it. He felt her give his hand a light squeeze and tug as she moved him toward a stationary shop, which here, in the ginza, would be a low key, enjoyable experience. He found the shy touch an incongruous act for the girl from the horseback dance but his being here with her was an incongruous act. Still, he enjoyed the touch, appreciated it. A mellow heat flowed through him. He knew Wild Bill would not be happy.

Chapter Thirteen Culpability

Back home, the squadron home, back on Okinawa, the Rock and outside rain was drizzling. The 1950's built BOQ was showing age. Tumble noticed a puddle from the leaking roof as he pumped two quarters into the vending machine. He chose a can of hot coffee, Georgia brand with milk and sugar over a can of cold coffee with the same. Not bad, not good, just coffee, too sweet, but any coffee was better than no coffee. It was 0530, a late spring morning. The days coming atmospheric conditions telegraphed themselves. It was already hot and humid. It would be hotter and more humid. Tumble finished his coffee and walked out of the BOQ. He had time for a base circling solo run and he looked forward to it. The run would be the high point of his day.

He started the run easy to warm up as he went along. The first half would be on pavement and the grass beside the road. The last portion was on a dirt and gravel road, the habu trail, through the elephant grass on the back side of the runway. The namesake habu was a small, local, quick, deadly snake rumored to inhabit the tall grass. Even if the habu was not there the area looked snaky and watchfulness was an asset.

The drizzle stopped but the humidity settled on Tumble's bare back like damp gauze. In less than a quarter mile the sweat rolled from his body in flat sheets and soaked his running shorts. The soothing flow of the run relaxed and massaged his mind and peace flowed through him as the sweat flowed over his body. He loved it. Nirvana would come in the stretch, there on the back side of the run. There, where he would be pleasantly tired, all extraneous thought pushed from his mind, his body in the rhythm of conditioned motion. It would be good, as good as anything else in his personal life. No the runner's high would be better than anything in his personal life. He did have the Marine Corps and he had flying. This was the peak of the day.

Punctuality was a personal fetish. He was in the squadron area by 0730. He was not on the day's flight schedule. Today would be a time to catch up on the ground job. Tumble climbed to the second deck of the hangar. The squadron administrative spaces and ready room were located there.

He topped the ladder well and saw Wild Bill coming toward him from the ready room with a cup of coffee. Tumble gave the appropriate greeting of the day as they passed. Wild Bill looked through Tumble and did not acknowledge the greeting. He walked to his office, the commanding officer's office.

Tumble shrugged. Wild Bill was obviously preoccupied and a CO is always given room for eccentricities.

Tumble walked into the ready room and direct to the coffee mess area. He picked up the Victor china mug with his name, aviator wings, and squadron patch on it. Many marines topside left their cups hanging on a hook board, in the coffee mess area, at the end of the working day. Tumble poured his coffee and the aroma told him the coffee was recently brewed. Fresh and hot coffee could cover the sin of many a bad coffee bean. That would not be true if the coffee sat for a half hour.

Crusoe, a major and the squadron S-1, the administrative officer, joined him and poured a cup with only a nod to Tumble.

Crusoe, W.W. Robinson, walked casually and peered about the ready room. He checked the high back chairs and turned his head full left and right in a theatrical gesture. He stood so as to see the entrance to the ready room. They were alone. He brought the coffee to his lips and held the cup there, looked Tumble in the eye, sipped and brought his cup down to just above his belt line.

"You have a 1000 appointment at Camp Adams legal. See Captain Choi. He's up on this and he is their best defense attorney," said Crusoe.

"What are you talking about?"

"Friday made the appointment for you as soon as she heard what was up."

"Friday?"

"Friday, my wife. She is the admin officer for Camp Adams legal."

"I know that."

"So be there."

"What the hell are you talking about?"

"You don't know?"

"Guess not, Crusoe. I don't have a clue."

"You know who Jenifer Masterson is?"

"Sure, I see her column. She is an investigative reporter, muckraker, has the Marine Corps and the government squirming on a regular basis. Screws it up half the time but she is entertaining. Loves misuse and abuse of government funds type stories."

"That is correct. You know who Major General Smallwell is?"

"The Inspector General for the Marine Corps."

"He is on island."

"Yes?"

"Two letters were sent back around Christmas and that explains the slow pace. One letter was to Masterson and one was to the IG. Masterson saw the cc and contacted the IG's office to confirm what was in her letter. Of course, they said they were hot on it, had to find their letter. Anyway, now they are hot on it. The IG himself is here with an investigative team."

"My part?"

"Misuse of tactical aircraft. You carried senior officers and top NCOs on a pheasant hunting trip. You, Captain MacFarland, canceled training to accommodate the hunters' schedule."

"Just doing what I was told. Who wrote the letter?"

"The powers that be think you wrote the letter. They think you are not smart enough to know you were putting yourself on report. I know you received verbal orders but the printed flight schedule shows nothing about flying to Cheju-do and certainly not three times."

"I wrote what we did on the flight log synopsis."

"So you did. That would be termed an admission. See Captain Choi at 1000. You will be glad you did. Friday says you are being hung out to dry. The idea is to catch you at the end of the day, a bit tired, not as mentally alert. Around lunch we'll be notified that you are to report to base legal at 1600 and you will be interviewed by the investigative team then."

"WTF, over."

"That's right. You figure. Wild Bill wants to be a bird and the group CO wants a star. They have to be men on horseback, men of decision. The easiest way, in peace time, to show you are not afraid of awesome responsibility is to execute one of your own and then sadly cluck over the necessity of the hard decision."

"Bullshit, Crusoe. They are Marine Corps officers."

"And about to undergo a gut check."

"They will do fine."

"Right now your career is the bet, buddy. Not theirs. See Choi. Don't be late. He's the best over there and once he talks to you they will have a hard time assigning him to a kangaroo court."

"Bullshit."

"You wish."

Discretion is often the better part of valor and Tumble remembered how Wild Bill had looked through him. Wild Bill, combat marine, solid commanding officer of a flying squadron, good pilot, one of the boys at the bar, ran with more girls than any two lieutenants. No, he might be a jerk but he would not run scared just for a promotion. Still, best to be prepared; hear what Choi knew; keep the appointment. It is not good to be the seventh man, the standing man, in a room with six chairs.

Fifteen minutes early Tumble walked into Camp Adams legal. He saw Friday across the room and she barely looked up at him. He checked in with the corporal at the reception desk. No waiting; he was sent in to see Captain Choi.

"So, you are the infamous outlaw, Captain Meriwether Lewis MacFarland the third," said Choi. He leaned back in his chair and propped a foot on an open lower desk drawer. He reached down and pulled a can of snuff from the top band of his black sock. "Friday tells me you are clueless," he said as he dropped snuff behind his lower lip.

"I cannot disagree with that."

"Please, sit down and we will talk. There is a lot to talk about. Captain, you are being investigated for misuse of Marine Corps aircraft, specifically a KC-130 on three separate occasions. You canceled a scheduled mission essential for the support of an exercise vital to national interest."

"Sounds a bit much and I did not fly anywhere I was not told to fly."

"Do you understand culpability as it pertains to this matter?"

"Must not."

"If an individual anywhere in the line of responsibility sees that an undertaking is in violation of correct, of legal, of authorized use of government property then that individual is required to put a stop to that misuse. More than one person may be culpable, but as the aircraft commander, you are culpable. Right now the others involved are pleading ignorance. They claim you did not properly inform them of the negative training impact, the canceling of in flight refueling qualification periods. Said requal periods were to ensure Marine Hornet aircrews were prepared to support an exercise vital to national interest, an exercise in support of freedom for all nations on the high seas. Frankly, when you see it in writing it makes you look like a criminal idiot."

"I explained the problem to the CO and to the horse holder for the pheasant hunters. The squadron gave me orders for each of those flights."

"Verbal orders?"

"Yes."

"Were they direct from Lieutenant Colonel Hitchcock?"

"No, the phone conversations were with the S-3, squadron operations officer, Major Mann, Sailor Mann."

"Right now Major Mann is just behind you on the IG depth chart. If they need two in front of the firing squad he will be the second. I have not seen a copy of the letter of accusations. Do you have any idea who would write such a letter?"

"No."

"Think. I am not sure this was aimed at you."

Tumble inhaled deeply and then exhaled. He watched Choi watch him. The thought drifted in slowly like a sail coming over the horizon.

"I have a guess and that would be the loadmaster, a fine marine sergeant, Hostile Lopez. He was discharged soon after the Cheju-do flights. He saw what a goat rope the whole thing was and was present on the flight deck when the horse holder, Lieutenant Colonel Ludlow, and I had words. He was also present when I told Ludlow what schedule we could accommodate without canceling any training. The CO struck Lopez with his cover upon our return from that last pheasant hunter flight."

"Was the striking of Sergeant Lopez reported or logged or somehow noted?"

"No, nothing official."

"Yes, I could see a young sergeant, humiliated by his CO and on the way to the world and his next life writing this. I suspect he liked you and thought he was helping you. Report the brass, make them sweat. He did not mention his humiliation in the letter. He probably never considered you would be first in line for the trouble."

"You are assuming the CO will not back me on this."

"Safe assumption. He was interviewed yesterday and you are here today. Here is what we shall do. This afternoon the IG investigators will come hard at you. You will be threatened with a court martial and while you are sweating that news a "good guy" will tell you there is a way out and that way is a resignation for the good of the service.

He will offer good paper. Everyone will be happy then, everyone but you. To give the court martial threat weight you will be read your rights, threatened with a less than honorable discharge. When that happens, when you are read your rights, you ask for me. Give them my card, and do not say a word until I arrive. Not one word. Don't ask for coffee. Do not make small talk. There is no small talk. This will be fun."

"For you."

"That's right, for me. See you this afternoon."

Tumble returned to the squadron. He was angry and a bit scared. Still, he wanted to talk to Wild Bill, his commanding officer. Part of a CO's job was to take care of his own.

Tumble took the ladder well two steps at a time. He topped the last one and saw Wild Bill and the XO, executive officer, Crazy Cal standing in the passage way. He walked up to them and waited to be acknowledged. The CO looked at him, no smile or pleasantry.

"Sir, may I have some of your time? I need to discuss a problem."

"Captain MacFarland I do not have time to talk to you," said Wild Bill. He turned away, walked into his office and closed the door.

Tumble turned to C2 who gave him a big smile and patted him on the shoulder.

"Have a nice day, Tumble," C2 said and walked away.

C2 was certifiable but the CO had just told Tumble he was in big trouble. Tumble dragged his confidence down the passageway.

"This is not good," Tumble thought, "and it is too bad. I like being a marine."

"Partner, you are down. Come, talk with me. I have something you can use," said Bongo.

Tumble was sitting on a storage foot locker in the back of the operations cubby where the lieutenants worked. He was drinking coffee as he waited for the inevitable summons. He looked up at Bongo.

"Know what these are?" Bongo said. In his left hand he held a dozen or more yellow sheets of paper and in his right hand white sheets of paper.

"They look like flight record synopsis. What an aircraft commander fills out at the end of each flight," said Tumble.

"Correct, Captain MacFarland, correct, but more than that as far as you are concerned."

"Oh?"

"I have gone back through the last few years of these reports and what I see is interesting," Bongo said and he handed the yellow sheets to Tumble.

Tumble took them and turned them over. There, on the back of each, in long hand, was a brief statement of the mission as flown. The statement was written and signed by the aircraft commander. What he saw was a record of no less than a dozen trips to Cheju-do in the past four years and two of the flights listed the current wing commanding general as a passenger. The CG was known for his love of a good time.

"We would have to dig to show training disrupted for these flights but I am working on that and expect success. That almost does not matter. I don't think the CG wants to be drawn directly into this. No one else wants him there either. Even if he was hurried on his way he would still have the opportunity to write or comment on the fitness reports of all of the officers involved. Wild Bill doesn't want that, the group CO doesn't want that and I doubt the IG wants the Marine Corps embarrassed at the major general level," said Bongo.

"You are smart for a lieutenant," said Tumble.

"I am smart at any level."

"Ok, I need these reports," said Tumble.

"You can't keep these," said Bongo holding up the yellow sheets. "They are unclassified but they are official government records and they are serialized. There is a record of the number."

"Copies?"

"Ahead of you. Three collated copies of the reports."

"Three?"

"Minimum you will need. One copy for your lawyer, one copy is yours and I would suggest you immediately send one copy off island. Send it to someone you trust."

Tumble took the white sheets.

"Thanks, Bongo. I'll be back after lunch."

"Good luck. You know I'll speak up for you."

"Be careful with that. You have a career opportunity here. Leave or stay, make that your choice and not theirs."

Tumble drove the Blue Bird back to his BOQ. He pulled the ice tray from the old refrigerator freezer and emptied the ice. He carefully folded one copy of the flight records, double sealed them in two plastic sealable bags, squeezed the air out, and put them in the bottom of the ice tray with a paper weight holding them down.

He added a film of water, not covering the paper weight. Later, he would work the paper weight out and fill that hole with water and freeze a second time. He addressed an envelope to a first cousin in Moultrie, Georgia and loaded in the third copy. He drove to the post office and mailed the copy with a letter that simply asked the contents be safely kept.

Somewhere in the trip to the BOQ and back to the squadron spaces a cold anger came over him. The anger had been slow in coming. Now, the more he thought about the issue the angrier he became. When he had first heard the situation, only that morning, he had not comprehended, and then he had not believed. When Choi had said, "when they read you your rights" he had still not believed the gravity of the situation. He had not been thinking. Then the CO had denied the request of one of his officers to speak with him, unthinkable under almost any circumstance. Now he was thinking.

He ran topside, went to the copier and made another copy of the flight records. He walked to the CO's office and the adjutant told him the CO had left for lunch at the Camp Adams Officers Club. The XO, Crazy Cal, was flying. Tumble could not make himself wait. He was angry with the CO, at what he perceived was a failure in leadership. He knew the Ops O, Sailor Mann, would be able to contact Wild Bill and Wild Bill was at Camp Adams, covering his own six and, most likely, polishing the plot to sacrifice Captain Tumble MacFarland for the good of the service or the CO's career which, to Wild Bill, was the same thing.

Tumble walked to the operations office, the S-3 office. He saw Sailor working at his desk. Someone had to do the daily drudgery. He lightly rapped the door post.

Sailor looked up and gave a tight smile.

"Got a minute?" said Tumble.

Sailor remained silent and gestured toward a vacant chair. He did not like to be interrupted when he was working.

"What's up?" said Sailor after Tumble sat but did not speak.

"Not much."

"That's good."

Tumble knew then that there was not an IG appointment in the immediate future for Sailor. He was totally in the dark as to his situation.

"Sailor, we have an issue."

"Oh?"

Tumble placed the flight record copies on the corner of Sailor's desk. Sailor picked them up and read them. He paused afterwards, sat looking at them and then looked at Tumble.

"I was at Camp Adams legal this morning, talked with a defense attorney. This afternoon I will be told to report to legal for what is called an interview. It is more than that. I will be threatened with court martial then, as an alternative, I will be offered an opportunity to resign for the good of the service. The charges will revolve around misuse and abuse of government property in that I canceled vital training missions to use a KC-130 to transport personnel on a morale and recreation trip. Evidently, I did not tell anyone up my chain of command about the problems, left the command uninformed."

"I will tell them I told you to go. I will tell them I talked this over with the Commanding Officer and those were his instructions."

"There is room for two in front of a firing squad. Better see how it goes with the IG team this afternoon. You may need your own Choi appointment. My request is for you to give those copies of serialized flight records to the CO. He can share them. We have taken the air wing commanding general and other general officers and personnel on the Cheju-do trip several times over the past few years. It is either ok or it is not. Bottom line: I may go down for this but I will not go alone. Not a threat, a fact."

"You sure?"

"Nothing to lose."

Tumble reported to Camp Adams legal at 1545 for his 1600 scheduled interview. Finally, at 1730, a sergeant approached him.

"Sir, your interview is postponed. You will be informed when to report. You may go."

"Thank you, sergeant."

The reaction was in the range of Tumble's expectations. The inquisitors would be mulling over the flight records now and trying to keep a lid on the general officer flights. Actually, Tumble did not think there was a problem with the flights. The crews had to fly to remain proficient and, if the flights did not interfere with higher priority missions, a flight to Cheju-do was as good as any. Still, if Tumble made an issue out of them, if Jenifer Masterson published them it would not be pretty. If that came to be someone higher ranking then a captain would have to be sacrificed. It was a dilemma for the men on horseback.

A week passed and Tumble was not called for an interview. Wild Bill ignored him. The only flying he did was the post maintenance check flights in the local area. He doubted he would have gotten those if the squadron was not short on pilots.

C2 was as genial as ever and called Tumble into his office. "Good news, bad news," he said.

"Yes sir?"

"We have to send someone to a staff assignment at Sakura. CO is assigning you. It is career broadening. We work up there enough you will be able to fly with us and stay current. Pack your bags and we fly you up in the morning."

They were stashing him out of sight and out of mind. C2 did not know the nature of the job. Was there a vacancy for a towel inventory officer?

"Better make new plans for the rest of my life," Tumble thought.

The next morning Tumble went to the squadron to pick up his orders. The Sakura flight was at noon. He was surprised when the adjutant came to him and told him to report to Wild Bill. He was not expecting a farewell.

Tumble decided this was a formal report. When bidden to enter the CO's office he stepped through the hatch, centered himself in front of the CO's desk, assumed the position of attention and reported in accordance to formulae.

"Sir, Captain MacFarland reporting as ordered."

Wild Bill took his time before looking at him. Tumble saw nothing in Wild Bill's eyes, except possibly, a hint of a smile.

"Captain, I have written two fitness reports on you. One is your regularly scheduled fitrep which is due this month. The other is a change of reporting senior and it is required because you are leaving my command."

Tumble remained silent and at attention. He had not been given his ease. He saw Wild Bill place two fitness reports on top of the desk and turn them in his direction. Covering three-quarters of each was a blank, white sheet of paper. The bottom portion of the fitrep where his name and social security number were typed was all that was exposed. Wild Bill was actually smiling.

"The only requirement on a fitrep brief is for you to confirm the correctness of your name and social security number in section C. Confirm the correctness and sign."

Tumble obeyed and Wild Bill dismissed him. He made an about face and left the office.

Tumble walked to the KC-130 that would carry him to MCAS Sakura. He carried all he owned in a sea bag and an old B-4 bag. He threw them under the 3,600 gallon fuselage fuel tank and went to the flight deck. Crusoe was the aircraft commander.

"Hi, Tumble," Crusoe said. "We get leveled off and you and I will have a conversation."

"Sounds good, mind if I help myself to the coffee?"

"Go ahead."

Tumble straddled the open galley deck over the flight deck ladder. In flight the hinged floor was dropped into place making the area a small galley. The coffee was in a heated and insulated jug made to fit in a designated niche. Chow hall coffee but he was use to it even though it was a bit weak. He reached into a flight suit pocket and took out a packet of instant coffee. He shook half the packet into his jug coffee to up the octane rating. He took his coffee into the back and sat on a red sling seat awaiting takeoff. When Crusoe wanted him he would know.

A half hour after takeoff Tumble heard the change in the prop sound as the Herc settled into cruise. A few minutes later Crusoe came down the ladder well. He paused at the bottom and two cups of coffee were handed down to him. He made his way to Tumble; took out his own packet of instant coffee and shook half into Tumble's cup and half into his.

"You are so screwed," said Crusoe.

"Figured so."

"Well, at least the term court martial is no longer on the table. Saw your fitreps when we did them in S-1. They are brilliant in concept and execution, uncontestable, and a shaft."

"Not surprised."

"Yep, two areas of the many areas on a fitrep have to be perfect for an officer. One is loyalty and the other is personal appearance. Anything less than half way up the scale in any area requires a special explanation by the fitrep writer and the mark is contestable at headquarters at the board of corrections. Any mark in the upper half flies. I mean you are excellent in loyalty and in personal appearance. Unfortunately, outstanding is better and you are not outstanding. There are several fitrep areas, in fact most of them, where excellent would be acceptable and you would still have a fighting chance for a career, for promotion. However, loyalty and personal appearance are not found there. Those have to be outstanding marks."

"No wonder the CO did not show me the report."

"Probably felt a little guilty. He knows he is covering his own ass at your expense. He still has hopes for full colonel."

"Nothing I can do?"

"Not that I know about. I just wanted you to know. A RIF, a reduction in force, is coming and a lot of officers will be forced to leave. You meet the promotion board next year and the way that works is the top twenty per cent get a thumbs up first pass. The bottom twenty per cent and, with these fitreps, that is you, get a thumbs down first pass. Your two recent fitness reports make easy work for the board unless you know someone on the board who will speak for you. That bottom twenty will be first out the door."

"Thanks. I'll think it over. I am regular Marine Corps and my obligation is up soon. I can resign anytime. My resignation would be one of dozens and no special stigma would be attached now. I'll give this some time and see if the pond scum settles. I had imagined myself as a career marine. I like it here."

"Good luck. Semper fi."

"Yeah, semper fi."

Chapter Fourteen White Elephant

Tumble checked in at the Sakura BOQ and was given temporary quarters until a permanent personnel room was available. He showered, touched up his alpha greens with a steam iron and lint tape and walked to headquarters.

The personnel officer, a mustang captain, a prior enlisted marine, looked over the orders, consulted his notes and told him he was assigned to the MALLO, Marine Expeditionary Force Air Lift Liaison Office. He was to report to Lieutenant Colonel Marlowe. The mustang handled the procedure with professional courtesy and sent Tumble on his way.

Tumble walked into the MALLO office and looked around. The only lieutenant colonel he saw was wearing Air Force blue.

"Sir, I am Captain Tumble MacFarland. I am to report to Lieutenant Colonel Marlowe."

"You are," said Marlowe with a smile. "Good to have you. We need another officer. I am on a joint tour and understand air logistics but I don't always understand marine speak. We work for the MEF-4 who is Colonel Lester. He is back in DC at Headquarters Marine Corps and will return in a couple of weeks. You'll be snapped in by then."

"Yes sir," said Tumble. He immediately liked Marlowe and hoped it would last, not that it mattered. He noticed the use of the marine term "snapped in," a term from the rifle range. It was not a common Air Force term. Tumble was pleased to have a real staff job. He had expected an exile job normally given to a yard bird private.

There was a lot to do at the MALLO. Air transport big and small was coordinated from there. He worked with the Marine Pacific Forces Command air office in Hawaii to funnel the requests and coordinated with the Marine Air Groups and with the Air Force transports when they were in theater. There was always an exercise or real world event requiring air lift. The coordination for the shooting part of air was done from operations and not logistics. Before a week of twelve to fifteen hour days was over, with the help of an experienced staff sergeant, Tumble thought he had a reasonable understanding of the duties and workings of the MALLO.

"What have you got on front burner?" asked Lieutenant Colonel Marlowe the second Wednesday in the office.

"All back burner stuff that I am trying to keep off the front," said Tumble.

"It'll wait. Leave, go. I'm impressed and you don't need to stay any longer today. The long days will come. I am going home and play with the baby's mama. You take the evening off."

"I can do that," said Tumble. He had already secured the staff sergeant and the corporal.

Tumble put his paper work away. It was still light outside.

Two hours later, after his first run since reporting he sat in the Sakura O Club bar. His company was the bartender and the juke box and namazu the walking catfish kept in the aquarium behind the bar and to the left of the bourbon. He sat at a table near the bar, not close enough to invite courtesy conversation from the bartender. He could see the room and anyone who entered if he had been watching.

He was contemplating the beaded water droplets on the back of a green beer bottle when he felt the presence of another.

"Hi," said Jewel, "surprised to see you here. I did not notice any 130s on the flight line."

"Fired from that job. Have a seat. Beer or something else?"

"I'm here for the beer," she said.

Tumble signaled the Japanese bar tender for two beers.

"Late for a school teacher on a Wednesday night?"

"Yes it is. Lesson plans still to go. Hungry though and thought I would order some fried rice."

"Okay, one fried rice," Tumble said to the bartender when he dropped the beers off.

"Not eating?"

"Have not thought about it."

Conversation was slow but easy. Jewel ate and they drank two more beers.

"I have to work tomorrow," Jewel said. "One more beer and one more country song?"

"Okay," said Tumble.

"I buy this time," said Jewel.

"Why not? New day and new way."

They walked out of the Officers Club together. The awkward moment arrived when a gentleman would offer to walk the lady home. Jewel decided to short cut the moment.

"I'll see myself home," she said. "I feel very safe on base."

"See you around," Tumble said. It was not the same as a "see you again" and they both knew it.

"You don't find me attractive?" said Jewel.

"I do, but I have too many problems right now," answered Tumble.

"I'm a problem? Suit yourself, see you around," said Jewel.

"That was stupid," thought Tumble as they parted.

"MALLO, Captain MacFarland." It was half past coffee number three when Tumble answered the phone.

"Tumble? Shadow, calling from Pacific HQ, joint staff, airlift."

"It is a good morning here. How can we help the big headquarters?" said Tumble. It was unusual to be talking directly to Shadow. He knew the man, another Herc driver, a major, but they had never served together. He had heard Shadow was on a good deal tour in Honolulu but there was a Marine headquarters between Sakura and the joint Pacific HQ. Contact usually came from the in between headquarters, the Marines.

"I talked to Nacho at lunch today. You know Nacho?"

"Sure, I talk with him regularly. He is my direct headquarters contact."

"He ran something by his boss and they gave me the ok to call you. They know all they want to know."

"Is this legal?"

"Mostly, it is not funded however."

"And?"

"We have a white elephant, a holy elephant, a sacred elephant, not sure what to call it. We have to move the elephant from Thailand to Sri Lanka."

"Isn't that an Air Force job?"

"Not without funding it isn't. The Air Force doesn't go anywhere without the money up front. In this case there is no money."

"A little more detail would help before I commit what is left of my career."

"The four-star admiral at PAC has some smoozing responsibilities in the Pacific region. Recently, in Bangkok, he made a happy hour promise. The Thais have, literally, a white elephant. The white elephant is considered rare and sacred. The Thais have more than one now and they promised their spare sacred elephant to Sri Lanka. Transportation is the problem or was until the admiral assured them he would get it done."

"The plot thickens."

"Yes it does. I went in at the back of the room this afternoon. We went to explain the lack of discretionary airlift funding; maybe other problems. My two-star stood in front of the four -star admiral who was sitting at his desk. My colonel stood behind the two star and behind him my lieutenant colonel; behind the lieutenant colonel was me, the note taker. The admiral knew why we were there.

By the way, you don't often see this. When the four-star admiral looked up he ignored all of us but the two-star and he said to him: 'the next time I hear about this elephant I want to hear it is in Sri Lanka.'"

"That is when you say 'yes sir.'"

"It is. When we walked out my two-star looked to us and said, 'make it happen.' So, I am."

"What do you need from me?"

"I want a Herc navigation training flight from Okinawa to Pattaya Beach, Thailand and then to Sri Lanka and I want the Pattaya Beach to Sri Lanka leg to carry the sacred white elephant. How big is a sacred white elephant? How is it transported? You are already wondering these things. This one is small enough for a cage and the cage will fit in a Herc, or so I have been told."

"That's a good start. Getting a crew for Pattaya won't be a problem. Paying for the gas out of training should not be a problem. It is training. What is missing is per diem. Not for the officers but for the enlisted crew members. I have gas money but I don't have per diem dollars."

"Okay, done. I'll work the per diem from here and I will write a personal check if need be. Let me know when the squadron is on board and you have crewmember names so I can start the diplomatic clearance. This should be a quick approval. The Thais want their elephant sent and Sri

Lanka wants the elephant. I will send the details as soon as we hang up."

Tumble walked to Lieutenant Colonel Marlowe's desk and briefed him.

"Marines can do this?" Marlowe asked.

"Marines will do this."

"OK. I'll see that the CG is briefed. Keep me up to speed."

Tumble called Sailor Mann back on the Rock. Fifteen minutes later Sailor called him back with a ready to go in twenty-four and the crew list. Wild Bill was the aircraft commander.

Tumble sent Shadow a message and followed with a phone call.

"Glad you called," said Shadow. "I have a by the way."

"Oh?"

"Yeah, seems the admiral ordered a custom, hand built, roll top desk, some nice inlays I hear, while he was in Thailand. It should be finished by now. Have elephant flight pick it up and the next time you send a Herc to Hawaii, if you are sending one in the next two weeks, have the desk brought to Hawaii."

"Roger, understand. Schedule a flight to Hickam in the next two weeks."

"Don't forget the desk."

"You owe us."

"Put it on the tab. Tumble, thanks."

Over the course of the next few days, via message, Tumble followed the progress of sacred white elephant flight. The day after the arrival of the Herc in Sri Lanka, at 0945 Japan Standard Time, the phone rang at Tumble's desk. When he answered he instantly recognized the warble and hollow drum sound of a high frequency radio phone patch. In the background he could hear the external power cart for the Herc. Someone was at the aircraft and using the Herc's high frequency radio.

Tumble knew who had to be calling. It was 6:15 in the evening in Sri Lanka. He spoke the formulae, "MALLO, Captain MacFarland on an unsecure line. What can I do for you?"

"Standby for a phone patch," said the controller who was patching the call.

"Tumble, Bongo here."

"How's Sri Lanka?"

"Fine. Wild Bill asked me to call. He's at a soiree."

"Soiree?"

"Don't know what else to call it. I'll be heading back over as soon as this call is complete.

Good thing Shadow told us to bring evening mess dress. We're a hit."

"Glad you're having a good time. Why the phone patch?"

"Do you know what comes with a sacred white elephant?"

"I have a lot of guesses but help me out."

"A mahout."

"Mahout?"

"Yes, that's an elephant driver, elephant keeper and we brought one with us from Thailand. He did a great job keeping the elephant squared away. Little elephant, in a cage, but still an elephant, and as much pink as white but they like him here. Dressed in silk and jewels the last I saw."

"Take a picture. What about the mahout?"

"The mahout isn't part of the gift. He wants to go home, back to Thailand. We have been asked by the Sri Lankans to take him back to Pattaya."

"OK, do it."

"What about the extra per diem?"

"You're kidding?"

"No and that is the real reason Wild Bill told me to call you."

"The per diem will be covered."

"You don't have to call Shadow?"

"It is 0245 in Honolulu. I'll talk to Shadow later today. Take the mahout home. I'll start collecting bottles for deposits. Your per diem will be covered."

"Great. I'll tell Wild Bill. By the way, I think women look great in saris."

"I look forward to the details."

"Break, break. Terminate phone patch and thanks for the help," said Bongo.

Tumble heard the controller reply and the phone patch was terminated.

He wondered what the per diem was for Sri Lanka and Thailand. It didn't matter. He was all in and Shadow was all in. "Make it happen" was the order and they were doing that. Sounded like another visit to the culpability zone.

Tumble went looking for Lieutenant Colonel Marlowe to keep him up to speed. He had been called into the commanding general's office an hour ago. Staff Sergeant Ferguson said Lieutenant Colonel Marlowe was still with the CG. Strange enough to make Tumble wonder what that was all about.

"Captain MacFarland, you are out of here," said Lieutenant Colonel Marlowe.

Tumble looked up. Marlowe did not sound angry.

"Sir?"

"Just when I could use you. Your squadron is short of pilots and we have a real world NEO shaping up."

"NEO?"

"Non-combatant evacuation order."

"Where?"

"Between Mindanao and Borneo there is a small island group near the Spratly Islands group I did not know existed. They have oil or maybe the sea bed around them has oil. Not sure about that. Anyway, there are Americans and Brits working there, and we have a consulate or a consulate annex. The island people claim independence. Indonesia claims the island; so does Malaysia and Brunei. There is another party, evidently tribal, maybe Moro, maybe not, but they want to be in charge and the banditry has turned to revolution which means killing and with momentum the killing is not particular. The local government doesn't want to be responsible for the safety of our people. We want our people out of there and so do the Brits. They are working something out of Butterworth with the Aussies and Malaysians. Anyway, we'll take people from both countries. The Philippine government has given us permission to use the old Subic air base at Cubi Point. This could turn into a small scale

Rawanda genocide. Muslims and Hindus; one eats cows and the other doesn't, Jonathan Swift."

"Jonathan Swift?"

"Yes, 'Gulliver's Travels'. Break your boiled egg on the small end or the big end."

"I'll have to review that, sir."

"I always enjoyed English literature. I just couldn't make a living at it. Anyway, Captain MacFarland, your Herc squadron is in support of the operation. They are short of fully qualified aircraft commanders. There is a C-12 leaving in a couple of hours for MCAS Naha. Pack your flight gear and be on it. You are assigned temporary duty back to your old squadron. Written orders will follow by message."

Tumble was downstairs before he remembered his phone patch from Sri Lanka. He ran back up and briefed Marlowe.

"We may have to buy the mahout a ticket. You better hustle. The C-12 King Air is for you but not for long."

Tumble ran to the BOQ and packed. He stopped by the BOQ office to give them a heads up. He came out of the office located next to the Officers Club.

"Leaving without a goodbye?" said Jewel. She was walking into the Club. It was the lunch hour.

Tumble had noticed her but had not walked over. She had taken it as a challenge.

"Short notice TDY back to the Rock."

"Anything to do with the NEO?"

"I just heard about it. How do you know?"

"O wives and girl friends know first."

"I can believe that."

"Maybe I will see you when you return."

"Maybe."

Jewel moved closer. Tumble stepped back. She moved closer again and kissed him lightly and slowly, with slightly parted lips and a hint of more. She stepped back and smiled. "See you when I see you."

"I look forward to it."

"You should."

Chapter Fifteen Texas Manners

The C-12 crew taxied the King Air to the Herc squadron flight line at MCAS Naha. Crazy Cal was waiting for Tumble.

"Don't bother going top side. Throw your gear on double nuts. Maintenance is working a couple of items and you should be ready to test and go within the hour. Join me in Cubi as soon as you can. We should have the op order by the time you get there. Rent has already worked up your flight plan and signed the ICAO for you."

"Yes sir, I can do all that."

"I am sure of it. There will be more for you to do when you reach the PI. Maintenance control has a fresh pot of coffee."

Tumble watched C2 walk away dragging his bouncing red steel, coffee can dog screeching across concrete at the end of the parachute cord leash. The flight line crew stood at attention on each side of the Herc crew entrance door as C2 boarded and the sergeant in charge saluted and passed the dog in to C2. Tumble knew no one had ordered side boy honors for C2 but the young marines loved him, loved that he was eccentric, loved that he had secrets, loved he could run any of them into the dirt. Still, C2 was a good pilot and, except for the certifiable part, a good officer. Wild Bill was also a good pilot, maybe a great one. The young marines stood clear of Wild Bill and there would never be a voluntary and spontaneous formation of side boys in Wild Bill's honor.

Tumble went to his assigned aircraft, spoke to the air crew getting the Herc ready and went looking for Viking, First Lieutenant Leif Erikson, his copilot. He would have preferred Bongo but Bongo was in Sri Lanka ferrying a white elephant with Wild Bill. Viking was good, just not as experienced.

He found Viking on the far side of the parking lot where the PC smoking area was located.

"Give it up, Viking."

"What? Give it up? I get my PT like this. I must walk three miles a day coming out here."

"You ready for this?"

"I joined for this."

"Didn't we all?"

Forty-five minutes later Tumble put Viking in the left seat to fly the leg to Subic. Marine pilots fly transports from the left seat whether the aircraft commander or co-pilot. The co-pilot would be an aircraft commander one day. Tumble knew he would be working from the left seat on the NEO with Viking in the right on the radios. If the NEO was cancelled, a high probability, he could always fly the leg back to Naha.

When they taxied out Tumble noticed a flurry of activity around the three-engine, heavy lift helicopters the CH-53E Super Sea Stallions. He figured they were invitees, too. He wondered how long it would take a 53 to fly to the PI. There were two squadron cargo frame Hercs with low speed refueling drogues on the line and that could mean coordination with the 53s or not enough crews or trash hauling since the fuselage fuel tanks were not installed in the Hercs with the low speed helicopter drogues.

The night was when they reached Subic Bay. There is dangerously high terrain on three and a half sides and the runway, inland side of the bay, is just above sea level. Viking did a good job on the dog leg, final approach course intercept over Grande Island, in Subic Bay, to land on Cubi Point's single, 9,000 X 200 feet runway.

The squadron's faded gray KC-130s were neatly parked with the four propeller blades on each of the four engines dressed at 12, 3, 6, and 9 o'clock on each aircraft and between each aircraft. The first mechanic saw to the propeller alignment at the end of each flight. Tumble did not see the Sakura Hornets as they taxied to the line. That meant an aircraft carrier was being positioned for air cover and the only carrier in the area was the Bobby Lee. There was not an LPH, helicopter carrier, in the area so helicopters, though needed, would not be an option unless the 53s came down. The last of the

Frogs the CH-46s, usually at Naha, were on exercise in Korea and the V-22 Ospreys were deployed aboard the helicopter carriers along with the Harriers. The CH-53E was air refuelable but that required a low speed refueling drogue on the Hercules not the high speed drogue used by tactical jets. The Army had some special ops air refuelable Ch-47s in Korea and Tumble did not know where the USAF special ops assets were located. Given time all could be coordinated but this was a come as you are party. Tumble wondered who was planning the NEO. That could make all the difference.

Tumble and Viking left Rodeo doing his flight engineer duties and exited the Herc to find Crazy Cal, Folger, the can dog, and two lieutenants dragging a cooler of iced San Miguel Beer in brown bottles with painted white labels. C2 had not received the PC word on beer or C2 did not care what the PC word was. Beer for the boys and one for me was his decision.

"One beer per man. Don't know when there will be time for another. Probably not time now. Don't know when we'll fly but we'll be ready. Welcome to the former Cubi Point Naval Air Station where once there was the best Officers Club in the world," said C2.

Tumble imagined a sparkle or tear in C2's eyes. Maybe it was a memory of his lieutenant days. C2 had broken service so he could have been here at the tail end of the heyday before the Filipino government evicted the U.S Navy in a nationalistic statement.

"Your quarters are at The Legends Hotel, formerly the black shoe chief's quarters so they are good quarters. We have four jeepneys with drivers standing by for base transportation. Get some rest. Admin is in base ops or what was, formerly, base ops," said C2 pointing to a nearby white, two story building. He put his empty brown bottle in the white cooler and while his hand was there picked up another San Miguel Beer and did not wipe the granular crushed ice from it. One of the lieutenants was quick with a bottle opener as there is not a twist off cap on a San Magoo.

C2 put a good Philippine made cigar in his mouth. He grinned and walked away toward base ops as he searched his flight suit for a match.

"He probably has a tattoo that reads 'kiss my ass'," said Viking.

"Wouldn't that be great," said Tumble.

The marines spent the next two days on maintenance, equipment checks, and planning which, because of the lack of detail available, presented special problems. Tumble habitually woke early which was not the best habit for a night flyer but it was why they made coffee. He ran the road from the aircraft line near Leyte Pier, the end of the runway on his left, the beach on his right until he turned up hill on the paved road and past a thousand fruit bats hanging in trees near the old BOQ. Then, he ran up hill, still on paved road through tropical jungle, and humidity sufficient to support aquatic life, to the former Naval Hospital. On the way down he circled the front of the old BOQ and ran past an RA-5 Vigilante on a pole and painted with a free style psychedelic paint job. How the mighty have fallen Tumble thought each time he passed the big carrier jet from the golden age and now a poor static display.

Breakfast could be a treat, or not. The fresh pastries were always excellent and the coffee fresh, strong, and good. Tumble thought the waiter, in the hotel restaurant, was from the old U.S. Navy days and the waiter remembered them well. He had heard older pilots refer to Subic as "the land of not quite right" and that had been a mystery to him until his second morning at breakfast.

The waiter, older, small paunch, balding, efficient in dark trousers, white shirt and dark tie stood at the table while the number one boy, unbidden, poured coffee.

"We have eggs to order. The scrambled are good," said the Filipino waiter.

"Eggs over easy, bacon, potatoes, toast, mango juice, and more coffee," said Tumble.

"Yes, scrambled, bacon, garlic rice, toast, mango juice, and more coffee," said the waiter.

"No, eggs over easy, bacon, potatoes, toast, mango juice, and more coffee," Tumble repeated.

"Yes, eggs over easy, bacon, potatoes, toast, mango juice, and more coffee," said the waiter.

Tumble sipped his coffee. A few minutes later the waiter returned and placed his breakfast on the table. It consisted of scrambled eggs, bacon, garlic rice, toast, and mango juice. The number one boy refilled his coffee. The waiter smiled and asked if Tumble would like anything else. Tumble returned the smile and graciously admitted defeat. Yes, the land of not quite right.

A corporal navigator stood in the doorway, at 0155 and gave each crew navigator a TPC, big scale tactical pilotage chart, as they entered the briefing room. "Hang onto this. We have one per crew," the young marine said.

Just inside the room an older Filipino man stood with insulated coffee urns, china cups, and fresh pastry and fruit. Someone had their eye on the ball. That would be either the first sergeant or C2. There would be a special officers' coffee mess assessment to cover the expense. The black coffee was hot and tasted strong and fresh. It was a great start.

C2 stood at the front of the room with Rent, the senior squadron navigator, who had spent the last two days in map study and Sailor Mann the squadron operations officer who did not appear to have slept. C2 always looked tired around the eyes so it was hard to tell about him. Wild Bill was flying from Thailand after the mahout drop. He, most likely, would not arrive in time for the operation.

"We were told to be ready to go this morning but the word is no word on the go," said Sailor. "We're in touch with wing and they are talking to Honolulu and that is all I know. Probably some State Department people in on this and hopefully they are in the Pacific and not in D.C. Rent will lead the chart brief. You heard the corporal when you came in, the chart you have is all you get. We do not have more so take care of it."

Tumble looked at the chart. He saw a fish hook shaped island with flat terrain. Not a very big island but with this number of aircraft involved there must be a lot of people to be evacuated.

"Our primary intel source, Wikipedia, indicates this is the main island of a three island group in a wanna be nation in the Sundaland Islands. There is a 5,000 foot crushed coral runway at the tip of the hook. The main town, can't pronounce the name, is here, at the eye. The other two islands in this operation do not have runways on them. There is a compound on the second island where most of the expats are housed and a soccer field, probably sand or dirt. It is just across this half mile strait and your chart shows the tip of that island but not the compound. Don't know anything about the last island," said Rent.

"The only difference between the Sundaland Islands and the nearby Spratly Islands is two of the three Sundaland Islands have potable water and, therefore, an indigenous population. The locals aren't the problem even though this is ostensibly an independence movement. There is a large oil and gas reserve in the area and now the islands are claimed as in rebellion, or a province or economic zone by China, Vietnam, Malaysia, Brunei, Indonesia, and Tumble's Uncle Sylvester in Hahira, Georgia.

We are not sure who is funding and supplying the instigators and thugs but they have a local boy who was educated in Singapore and England as a school teacher and he is the rebellion figurehead leader. The State Department is working the details so we can do a benign environment NEO and then step aside and let the local participants solve their own problem. We buy from the winner," Sailor said.

Tumble gave an obligatory smile at his acknowledged presence. Sailor was not known for humor and two attempts at humor at 0200 were worth note. He had not had a chance for a personal talk with Sailor in the last two days. This was Sailor's third consecutive Okinawa tour. He was the squadron duty expert on all things Pacific and was developing an epicanthic fold.

"Sir," Corporal Sami Jimenez, even in cammies the best looking admin corporal in the Marines, said. Officially, that thought was forbidden. However, Corporal Jimenez wearing bloused cammie trousers and an asset enhancing Marine green tee shirt made ignoring a challenge. Corporal Jimenez was standing at the door with a manila folder held before her. She was looking at C2 with excitement in her eyes. Everyone was looking at the corporal.

"Come in corporal," said C2.

Tumble knew C2 had called an all lieutenants meeting with a special invite to a couple of captains soon after the corporal had checked into the squadron. He had told the young gentlemen, in unquestionable terms, their careers and lives depended on maintaining a strictly professional relationship with Corporal Jimenez. The warning had taken, mostly, as Bongo was the only lieutenant Tumble had observed who would joke with her.

In the library silence of the room C2 studied the paper from the folder. He returned the single sheet of paper to the folder, grinned, renewed the fire on his area forbidden cigar, and handed the folder to Sailor. Sailor read the paper and looked a bit more somber than C2.

Sailor looked at C2 who nodded back, pulled the cigar from his mouth, tilted his head up, exhaled a great cloud of fragrant blue cigar smoke and smiled at the overhead.

"The NEO is a go. We don't have a good count on the number of evacuees. Here is the basic plan. One Herc will carry what it needs to ground refuel the helos. Two cargo frames have low speed drogues if we have to in flight refuel the 53s. This should give us spare hoses. The first Herc on island will stay on deck to provide helo ground refueling, as necessary, and act as the command post. It will carry a platoon of grunts to secure the terminal area. The local police are guaranteeing the safety of the airfield. The grunts will ride herd on that. We don't have enough airframes for an overhead safety tanker. The 53s will work out of Palawan Province near Puerto Princesa. They will work the island with the expat compound and bring the evacuees to the airfield. A lot of this is make it happen planning. Be ready to improvise. We'll be running a Puerto Princesa shuttle. There is a long day in front of us.

Fire fights have been reported on the main island, rumors of summary executions but not confirmed. We don't know who is shooting who. There are several groups to choose from. We are going to pick up Americans and Brits and whoever else we are told to take. Phone lines are down but there is comm via Skype with the expat community and the consulate annex and they are screaming. The local security is still hanging in. So far no one has assaulted their positions but that can change at any time," said Sailor.

Sailor continued with the details of the plan and asked for questions. Before he could get to them Crazy Cal held his cigar hand in the air and stood.

"Well, well, it is a go. Half my philosophy of life comes from Louis L'Amour westerns. You ride for the brand and give a day's work for a day's pay; more than one kind of pliers cuts wire. In other words, you have the basics of the plan. Count on surprises. Most of this we'll have to pull out of our asses. Don't do anything stupid, at least not too stupid. Don't leave any marines. Don't fuck it up.

We didn't come armed. I don't send anyone unarmed into harm's way. See the two Filipino marines on the first deck when you leave. Our sea service friend has agreed to loan us side arms, Armscor Model 1911 .45s. Good pistol and see that it is returned," C2 said.

"Our marines are checked out with the Beretta M9 and not a .45," Viking said as they stood in line to sign for their weapons from the Filipino Marine sergeant.

"True, however, I own a 1911 and spend a lot of range time with it. Call a school circle when we get to the airplane and I'll give a quick and dirty and until then no one loads their pistol and even then no one chambers a round unless we are caught on the ground and need to shoot," said Tumble.

"Sure would like a couple of M-16s," said Viking.

"We don't know who the players are, who to shoot," said Tumble.

"I'm from Texas," said Viking.

"I know that. I never met anyone from Texas who did not say it as part of their name. You're worse than fighter pilots about bragging."

"Not bragging if it is true. Texas manners, if someone shoots at you then you owe them the courtesy of return fire."

"Ok but we have two boxes of ammo, a hundred rounds total, and two magazines each for six men. That is 7 rounds to a magazine, 84 rounds to load all plus 16 left over. We'll depend on the grunts for area security. The pistol is in case the situation turns personal."

Chapter Sixteen NEO

They flew south-south-west and dawn was a rumor at their back. The stars in the night sky were twinkling like lines described in a nursery song. Oil platforms in the blackness of the Sulu Sea and west gave fuzzy, glowing, yellow pin pricks of light as they burned off natural gas and other duller gray-white and blue-white surface lights came from inter island shipping and night fishing boats. Tumble was unsure how many of the small islands were inhabited and, if they were, what light sources should be visible at 20,000 feet. He hoped someone had thought to keep the sky clear. He did not want to meet a DeHavilland Dash 8 on the red eye from Zamboanga to Kota Kinabalu.

"The island is at12 o'clock just coming onto radar," said Rent. "We're twenty minutes out from our start descent point."

"Thanks," Tumble said. He glanced down at his radar repeater scope and saw the ghostly green primary return. He changed his range scale to eighty. When the island hit the eighty mark he would begin descent. It was a little early but he wanted a chance to look the situation over. Crazy Cal would be in the descent. He would be first on deck. The grunts would pour out of C2's Herc and secure the position. The 53s should be somewhere under the left wing or maybe ahead, Tumble thought. They carried their own grunts for work on the two outlying islands where most of the evacuees were housed. The 53s coming in from Palawan would start the blue collar work ferrying the evacuees from the other islands to the airport where the Hercs were waiting but, hopefully, not waiting very long. No one was sure how many evacuees there were but the Hercs, even with a fuselage fuel tank, would be able to haul out a lot people and they would drop them at Puerto Princesa International Airport and come back for more. The short distance round trip was a force multiplier. There were diplomats, business people, oil platform workers, and maybe some families. C2 had briefed to load the Hercs standing room only so they would take all they could cram on each flight. C2 did not want a panic stampede on the last Herc out if the situation turned rough. Weight would not be the limiting factor. Cubic volume would fill that bill. Sounded like a plan but when does anything go to plan?

"Buckshot One on deck," was said on the radio ops frequency.

Good, C2 was there and it sounded as benign as could be with a strange field approach before the first trickle of dawn light. Even C2 must have had little beads of sweat running down his temples. Radar offset from the island shore line and landing lights on in close to ensure he was actually aligned with a 5,000 feet crushed coral surfaced runway. The grunts would be moving out of the aircraft and establishing a perimeter. C2's crew would be placing highway flares at the approach end of the runway. If they could find a vehicle they would use the headlights to mark the land abeam area. No GAIL lightening or night vision goggles. Dawn light would soon be there. Benign daylight extraction of non-combatants was the plan from the Potomac and the foot dragging and shoestring nature of the NEO made it obvious how much Washington had not wanted to do this. Under the circumstances it was the best that could be done.

C2 would taxi his Herc to the barely adequate sized crushed coral ramp that extended like a mushroom from the east end of the runway. On the ramp perimeter was a small tin roof terminal building. There, adjacent to the ramp, the crew would drag refueling lines from their Herc and set up a ground refueling station for the CH-53s using the Herc's external single point refueling panel. Other than C2's Herc there would be room for one other Herc on the ground.

The 53s had sent their own taxi directors and maintenance personnel with C2. Someone had learned from the disaster at Desert One during the 1979 Iranian Hostage Rescue attempt. Positive control for the landing and departing 53s would be provided by their own personnel and the Herc crew would run the gas station.

C2 would be the controller for the landing and departing KC-130 Hercules aircraft. The Hercs would turn around using the terminal ramp and hammerhead, drop the cargo ramp and open the aft cargo door and, with engines running, the evacuees would be loaded from the back. The CH-53s would land between the right wing of the in position Herc and the left wing of C2s Herc, unload and leave. When full and without a 53 on deck the Herc would takeoff. When refueling was required there would be a pause in the operation. The 53 would land forward and right of the Herc, there wasn't room parallel to the right of the Herc. The ground refueling would be done from the right side of the Herc. It was very tight quarters.

Tumble found the pilot's mantra, "don't screw it up," running through his head. In a few hours they would be heroes or zeros. He shook it off and compartmentalized, only the flying, only the mission. "Descent checklist," he said.

"Sir, we are at the start descent point," said Rent. Tumble noted the "sir" and it was a measure of tenseness and professionalism setting a tone for the crew that Rent, a Chief Warrant Officer-4, had not called him Tumble.

"Tell C2 we are out of twenty," Tumble said.

"Roger," said Viking and he made the call.

"Good to hear from you Buckshot 2. Land opposite direction from the original brief. This runway is not as wide as advertised. There is room for a turn around on the ramp. Winchester is a good altimeter. Calm winds, clear skies, no obstructions to visibility, 25C," said C2. Tumble knew C2 had rolled the numbers in the Kollsman window and at 30.30 the altimeter's indicated altitude agreed with the known field elevation, or at least the published field elevation which might not be the same thing. It was government work and close enough.

Passing 8,000 feet Tumble thought he saw tracer fire, flashing strobes of green light horizontal to the ground. Small stuff, nothing coming their way, probably not at the airport as C2 was silent. Maybe disco was back?

The random approach for small arms avoidance was briefed. It was the plan all along because you never knew what an armed, undisciplined force might decide to do with their new Kalashnikovs.

"Bleed air off," said Rodeo. It was a little extra engine protection.

Tumble spotted the flares marking the landing end of the runway. He reversed his start direction in the descent. The ground was darker than the sky, a black hole. He slowed to 180 knots and crossed the red flare line on a parallel course at 4,500 feet. He wondered who had walked the length and width of the runway to check the measurements.

"Flaps fifty," Tumble said.

He felt the rumble and shake of the Herc as the big fowler flaps moved aft and down. Tumble pushed the yoke and gave a couple of short nose down thumb strokes on the trim to override the tendency for the airplane to rise with the increased lift. He tweaked his power back the width of two throttle knobs and counted aloud, "one potato, two potato, three potato, four."

He reduced a bit more power and rolled the Herc into a left thirty degrees angle of bank descending turn. They came down between 1000 and 1200 feet per minute. He initiated a 180 degree turn at half his initial altitude as he came over C2's Herc and began to slow past 170 knots. Abeam the point of intended landing the landing zone was still in morning shadows. "Gear down and before landing checks."

Tumble heard Viking running the checks. He lost sight of the runway. He pulled his body forward and pushed his head toward the swing window to look out the left side of the cockpit and search for the runway end flares.

He saw them. The flares defined the end of the runway and he knew about where C2 was parked. There was no ground fire. He extended his downwind a few heart beats to make up for being close abeam then rolled through 180 degrees of turn to the no wind final approach course.

"Landing checklist complete," said Viking.

Tumble flicked his eyes back inside the cockpit cross checking airspeed, altitude, angle of bank, and rate of descent. He checked the gear down indicator and took Viking's and Rodeo's word for the rest of the checklist.

He was at five hundred feet, 140 knots and slowing, aligned with where he thought the runway centerline should be and what he judged to be a half mile from the end of the runway. There was a lot of educated guess work going on.

"One hundred flaps," Tumble called. The speed began to bleed off as the flaps went full down. The Herc felt as if a giant stood under the tail and pushed upwards sharply rotating the aircraft nose toward the ground. Tumble let the nose stabilize pointed down at the intended point of landing area. He gave a two heart beat left thumb pull on the nose up trim. He had held the landing lights extended and off but now he wanted to see the gray-white of the crushed coral runway. "Landing lights on," he said. Miracle of miracles there, before them, was the short, dirty ribbon of runway. He made a minor correction for line up and cross checked his airspeed. He crossed the flares slowing past 115 knots.

They were descending at 500 feet per minute rate of descent and they smoothly slammed onto the runway at 100 knots and 200 feet past the flares. Tumble pulled the throttles to flight idle then up and over the throttle quadrant gate to ground idle.

"Spinoff, ground idle," said Rodeo.

That was need to know information as a propeller stuck in the flight range would be a wild and unhealthy ride if the throttles in the ground range were pulled to maximum reverse. The statement confirmed what Tumble had felt. The 16 Hamilton Standard propeller blades had gone flat, providing a barn door slowing effect when they came into the ground range. He pulled the throttles aft and bumped max reverse as he applied the brakes. The big, light weight Herc sagged to a walk and Tumble came off the brakes and out of reverse. Coral dust swirled up into the maelstrom created by the reverse pitch props and settled on the Herc as it slowed through the vision obscuring dust bath.

"Clean it up and after landing checks," he said.

After sun up the marker panels would be out and the runway itself visible from a distance. Those would be good things. Tumble could see the brush shadows at the runway edge and the wing tips extended beyond the defined edge of the runway. C2 was right. Either the runway margins were not kept clear or the runway was not the advertised width.

"Taxi and wing lights off," Tumble said. There was no need to highlight his airplane and he could just make out the dirty gray runway. At the far end of the runway C2 had stationed a taxi director who was moving extended lighted wands down then straight up in the taxi straight ahead signal. The whole operation could be stopped if a Herc dropped a wheel off the runway into a hidden ditch. The straight ahead taxi director pointed his red lighted wands to Tumble's left and handed him off to another taxi director standing on the ramp.

The crushed coral ramp area with the tin roof terminal building hung like a coconut from a palm beyond the end of the runway. By landing toward the terminal they had not had to make a 180 degree turn on the runway. The terminal ramp offered tight turn around room. Tumble looked left toward the new taxi director. He saw a short taxi throat to the ramp at 45 degrees from the end of the runway. C2's Herc was parked tail toward the concrete block terminal and far to the offside of the parking ramp. He saw red intake plugs on C2's engines. They would offer some protection from all the coral sand, dust, and gravel being blown up by landing Hercs and helicopters. Care would be needed to keep prop blast to a minimum until runway aligned for takeoff.

He saw the red lighted flash light wands of the next marine taxi director. He was the first mech from C2's crew. The taxi director held both wands over his head and moved them straight down and up to signal Tumble to taxi directly toward the taxi director. The man brought them down the taxi throat and looked to his left. He dropped the left wand low and pointed to his left and began to bring the right wand, in a waving motion, from chest level to head level and he moved to his left. Tumble followed and the Herc made a right 45 degree turn which put it parallel and opposite direction to C2's Herc. The taxi director then brought them straight ahead toward the dark, ill defined ramp margin as far as he dared. He dropped his right wand low and waved with his left hand and Tumble turned his Herc 90 degrees left. The taxi director glanced over his shoulder and got a thumbs up and clear signal from a marine standing near the tail of C2's Herc. The taxi director broke into a double time run to his right, still with right lighted wand held low and brought Tumble into a hard left turn. The marine at the tail of C2's Herc sprinted toward the wing tip to provide assurance of clearance. The two Hercs were now parallel but that was not the plan. The taxi director gave the straight ahead signal then went to a short up and down, a double hand patting motion, the slow ahead signal. Then, still signaling slow so as to not inundate the other Herc with debris from prop blast, he gave another turn for Tumble to follow 45 degrees to the left then straight ahead which put the Herc back in the taxi way throat near the departure end of the runway. Now, there was adequate room to land a 53 between and aft of the two Hercs, ground refuel when needed from C2's Herc, unload the evacuees, and march them straight to Tumble's waiting Herc.

"If we're going to be a while we'll run the APU and shut 'em all down," said Tumble.

Rodeo acknowledged.

"C2 coming up, sir," said the first mech who was standing on the ramp in front of the Herc and monitoring the ICS.

Tumble looked forward in the dim first light of day. He saw C2 stop at the young marine first mech and speak to him while slapping him on the back hard enough to stagger the younger man. The marine grinned and snapped a thumbs up. Tumble noticed C2 was wearing glasses. He had never seen that before. C2 must be in his late 40s. He probably needed them to help his night vision. C2 had an unlit cigar in his mouth and what some called a vacant smile on his lips. Tumble figured it was effective camouflage. Tumble took his headset off and turned in his seat to see C2 climb to the flight deck.

"Good job, Tumble. There's a little shooting going near the town. Grunts are checking. We haven't seen any problems here. Had to bring you in like that. There's no room the other way. Don't need any big FOD damage. As it was I could hear coral sand like rain on a tin roof pinging off my airplane. With daylight we may figure out a better way. The 53s will land between us. The evacuees will be brought direct from the 53 to you. Have your loadmaster do a good head count. There will not be time for a manifest before takeoff. Get one on the way," C2 said.

He had spit the words out and the sentences were run together but they were clear to Tumble. C2's smile broadened the more he talked. Tumble realized Crazy Cal was enjoying this and so was he.

"53 inbound," said Viking.

C2 slapped Tumble and Rodeo on the shoulders and left the flight deck. He was walking fast as he went by the first mech and, without stopping, gave the marine a head high thumbs up. It was a good and natural leadership gesture that individually acknowledged the presence of the marine and his direct contribution to the mission.

Tumble could hear the whop-whop of the helicopter blades. "Before start check list. Get 'em all going."

"Here come the pax, sir. Bunch of 'em and looks like a couple of wounded, too," said the load master on the intercom.

"Ok. There should be another 53 right behind this one. We'll need that for a full load."

"Son of a bitch. What was that?" said Viking.

Tumble had not noticed anything. He turned to look at Viking who had poked his head out of his open swing window to see the 53 land.

"Something just streaked through the tail of C2's Herc."

"What?"

"Yeah, like a tube of fire. No explosion though. Everybody over there is on the dirt except for C2. He's talking on a hand held."

"RPG," said Rodeo.

"What?"

"Rocket propelled grenade. Didn't go off but punched a hole. Seen it before. No explosion. Thin skin or malfunction. Either way lucky," said Rodeo.

"Luck counts two points just like skill," said Viking.

"We got sixty-two aboard. Two wounded. Big 53 load," said the loadmaster.

"Probably have the seats up and everyone is sitting on the deck," said Tumble.

"Captain MacFarland," said a new voice. "I'm the corpsman off the 53. Got one hurt bad back here and we need a hospital ASAP. We need to go."

"Standby," said Tumble. "Viking, call C2. Give him the scoop."

"C2 says go. See you on the rebound."

"We're out of here. Close her up. Bleeds off, max effort takeoff. Viking, get me the numbers."

They took off west and turned east into the rising sun clean and Herc fast, also known as not so fast, toward Palawan Island and Puerto Princesa.

"Make sure the reception committee knows we are inbound with wounded," said Tumble.

"Working," said Viking.

"Marine? Load, the wounded, are they marines?"

"Yes sir and one looks bad. Corpsman is doing all he can do. This guy will be first off."

The Puerto Princesa landing was uneventful. They kept the engines running and were airborne again within fifteen minutes of touchdown. News of the wounded marines would come later. They passed Sailor headed in the opposite direction and were told the evac was going ok, nothing new.

The sun was full up on a bright, clear, beautiful morning and the sea was a clear tourmaline blue transitioning to emerald green at the khaki colored shoreline banded by the dark jade green of coconut palm fronds. The Herc crew could see all three islands as they set up for the second approach. Crossing the departure end of the runway to set up for a course reversal and landing small arms fire was reported from the palm shadows. Was it aimed at them? It was hard to tell at that altitude. There were people milling around east of the field. Tumble could not tell if they were armed or if they were trying to stay out of the way.

"Viking, check with C2. We're starting the approach." Tumble monitored the radio call while scanning his instruments and eyeballing the landing area.

"Clear as it will get. Keep an eye out and come on down," said C2.

The Herc was flown to hit the key at 4,500 feet for small arms avoidance but you can't stay there and land. Tumble maneuvered to stay inside the airfield perimeter which put him hanging full flaps, power back, speed falling away in clumps, and on a steep approach angle, aircraft attitude determined his airspeed. The idea was to run out of excess airspeed and altitude at the same time and to make a firm touchdown and a short landing rollout.

The Herc was descending 400 to 500 feet per minute for the assault landing and passing 75 feet above the runway and Tumble was judging an adjustment for touchdown when the cockpit window at Vikings feet splintered from heavy caliber ground fire. Viking was struck by fragmented, aluminum, window framing and shards of laminated, clear windscreen. He involuntarily arched and strained against his seat harness in protest as kinetic energy drove the splinters into his body. Tumble's right hand received a numbing blow and was lifted from the throttle quadrant as additional shards of window and pieces of aluminum peppered the cockpit. Tumble's right side was covered in blood but most of that was from Viking. The overhead T handle lights came on bright red, indicating fires in numbers three and four engines. The new sound was the air rushing through the recently made hole in the Herc cockpit.

Rodeo Simpson, covered with Viking's blood, reached forward and snatched Viking, his body in a spasm, off the control yoke. When Viking came away from the control yoke Tumble could see the hydraulic panel with the red and yellow utility hydraulic lights lit up like a Christmas tree. They complimented the overhead light show where the engines number 3 and 4 red firelights lit the overhead T-handles. A thousand hours of drill and study made the system information and required procedures as autonomous as breathing. Tumble knew he had lost half the hydraulics for his flight controls, all normal braking and nose wheel steering. His aircraft configuration, landing gear down and one-hundred flaps, had him past other problems.

"Engine fire confirmation from the back," said Rodeo who, with his right hand was holding

Viking's body against the seat back. The inertial reel for the seat harness had been cut and the inertial reel could not hold Viking in place.

"Let 'em run until we're stopped," said Tumble. They were Tumble's first words. They both knew how it had to go. Tumble had trouble gripping the blood slick throttles with his numbed right hand. Time seemed to slow as he placed his hand forward of the throttle knobs and used a fist and bent wrist to reduce power and to bump up the power, after he pulled off too much, he dropped his hand behind the throttle quadrant and tapped it forward. He could smell the odor of fresh blood, and open viscera mixing with an odor of overheated wiring.

Normal braking was gone with the utility hydraulics and there was not enough time to reach over and select emergency brakes on the instrument panel switch in front of Viking, if the switch was still there. They would have to go to max reverse on all engines which included the two that were burning. Get the Herc stopped, T-handles and fire bottles, alarm bell, and emergency ground evacuation. Trained aircrew members were aboard and they were expected to know what to do. Run away from the nose, into the wind, not parallel to fuel laden wings, and put some distance from the potential explosion and fire. There was no worry concerning being hit by a responding crash crew vehicle. There were none.

The touchdown was hard but no bounce. That was good. It dissipated energy in a hurry. The nose wheel touched down and, without utility hydraulics, twisted ninety degrees to the direction of travel. The nose tires pulled from the metal wheels and the wheels dug into the crushed coral runway surface. The nose wheel plowing down the runway caused the cockpit to shake violently.

Rodeo saw the problem with Tumble's right hand. He released Viking and reached forward from his center seat, grabbed the four throttles, pulled them up, over the detent, dropped them into the ground range and pulled them to reverse. The good news was the caster of the nose wheel helped the four reversed Hamilton Standard propellers quick stop the brakeless Herc. The reliable Allison T-56 engines, including the two turning and burning, fulfilled their mechanical duty driving the props at 100 per cent RPM.

Before the coral dust bloom engulfing the front of the Herc was full Rodeo was in his emergency flow pulling T-handles and shooting the fire retardant bottles, securing fuel and batteries. The extra holes in the aircraft ensured depressurization. Fuel burns and vapor explodes. If the fuel was contained the explosion might be avoided.

Tumble pulled all four engine condition levers to the feather position and reached to the left cockpit side panel and raised the red switch guard and toggled the alarm bell wired hot from the battery bus. Maybe superfluous given the situation but the loud ringing noise might bring a dazed marine to action and escape.

Rent was pulling Viking from the seat and using one hand to keep the intestines in place. Tumble popped the lock on his own harness and turned right to help Rent. In his hurry he smashed his head against the flight engineer's overhead panel. That Viking was dying Tumble did not doubt but the heart was still beating and blood, unconstrained by vessels, was pumping out of wounds, large and small with every heart beat and with each breath the pink lung blood frothed from Viking's lips and bubbled from his nose. The pupils were rolled out of sight and the white portion of the eyes bulged.

They dragged Viking from the seat and across the cockpit deck. Rodeo jumped down the ladder well to the cargo deck level and turned to take Viking's legs. Tumble and Rent manhandled Viking down and smacked the side of his head against the open and locked galley deck.

Tumble and Rent followed as best they could. In their hurry they scraped Viking's wounded, right rib cage against the crew entrance door frame. The three of them struggled for a better grip and balance and they carried Viking as fast as they could. They caught up with a corporal, the right observer, who was limping.

"Anyone left?" said Tumble. The sight of the young marine recalled him to his greater duty.

"Don't think so, sir. I gave a quick look," said the corporal.

"Take my place, marine," said Tumble.

The marine grabbed under the injured pilot's arms.

"Count yourself, numb nuts, count yourself. You'll never get the right answer if you do not count yourself." The screaming words were etched in his mind from when his sergeant instructor, at Quantico, had screamed them a half inch from the front of Tumble's spittle bathed nose.

Tumble held his blood covered right arm up, stabbed his chest with his thumb, counted aloud, "one," and pointed his index finger and counted aloud each marine he saw running from the Herc.

The count was short by one marine. That did not mean the marine was in the Herc nor did it mean the marine was out of the Herc. The count did mean Tumble had to return to the Herc. He was the aircraft commander, the marine officer responsible.

Tumble turned and stepped off in the direction of the Herc. The explosion came from the right wing of the Herc. Black oily smoke and Halloween orange flame rose up and the burst seemed to draw the right wing into the air before dropping it back to the runway. The noise was a deep bass woof and the hot air over pressure rolled out from the explosion like a tsunami induced wave. It caught the fleeing marines from the rear, washed over them and knocked them to the ground. Tumble was facing the explosion and he felt the instant, searing heat on his face as he was driven to his back.

Tumble rolled off his back and onto his knees, lifted his head and saw the fireball had spread across the Herc to the other wing and was mushrooming dirty and black and yellow into the beautiful, early morning sky. There was a second explosion. It was not as bad as the first when it came and he was already on the ground. Fortunately, they were outside the lethal range of the heat and the shock wave which was not the same as outside the harmful range. Tumble was mesmerized and helpless for a heartbeat. He rose up dazed, then staggered back toward the group carrying Viking. Those marines had been several yards further away from the explosion. They were up and moving.

He saw C2 helping with Viking and a corpsman shouting instructions. They put Viking on the ground under a tin awning that formed the roof of a dirt floor porch at the terminal building. The young petty officer, a Navy corpsman, had come to help evacuate civilians, care for sprains and breaks, dehydration and frightened people. Now, he needed a trauma surgeon's skills to care for the grievously wounded officer though even those skills would be insufficient.

Rent unzipped his flight suit to his waist and stripped off his marine green tee shirt. He pointed at Tumble's right hand. Tumble glanced down and saw a stub of bone where the little finger of his hand had been. The blood from it was dropping onto the toe of his flight boot. Tumble nodded at Rent and Rent used the sweat wet tee shirt to tightly wrap

Tumble's hand. The corpsman was too busy to be bothered.

"Do you have a good count of your marines?" said C2. He had his right hand on Tumble's left shoulder, lightly shaking it, and looking him in the eyes.

"No sir."

"Get one," said C2. Tumble must have passed C2's situational assessment. He gave Tumble's shoulder a firm squeeze and gently shook the shoulder. He ignored Tumble's tee shirt wrapped hand and heat blistered face.

"Yes sir," said Tumble. He was feeling the throbbing pain in his hand now and what felt like a bad, bad sun burn on his face and the aftermath of the crash landing or was it a shoot down? The damaged hand would have to wait. He had to fake composure and execute his duty. In the distance, beyond the terminal building, he heard heavy machine gun fire, a 12.5 mm or a ma deuce .50 cal. It was not in a position to be the weapon that had stitched his Herc just prior to touchdown. That meant more than one heavy machine gun. He was not sure who was being fired upon. He saw most of his crew near the terminal building where Rodeo Simpson had gathered them. He walked over and looked each man in the face before he counted him. He had flown with all the men here. The one's from C2's crew and from his and he had to keep them separated in his mind to make the count work. His count was one man short.

Rent placed a hand on Tumble's shoulder and making a full hand palm vertical gesture with the other hand motioned down the runway. A man in a flight suit was there. The man stumbled to his knees and looked back toward the burning Herc.

Tumble started toward the man and was caught up short by C2, "your weapon, Captain. Take it out of the holster."

Tumble complied. The pistol was awkward in his left hand. He failed to chamber a round. Rent followed and they moved toward the marine. He was the loadmaster, a man new to the squadron. He was dazed but held an aircraft first aid kit in his left hand. His right forearm, held down, was turned wrong; bone protruded through the skin and blood soaked his flight suit from the waist down. Rent helped the man to his feet.

Tumble watched the brush and palm line beyond the airfield limits. The gun that had hit them had been about 200 meters out. Maybe truck mounted. That meant, most likely, the three of them could be seen where they stood. The shooters, perhaps stunned by their spectacular success, were inactive at the moment.

The man grunted as he stood and forced a tight smile. They began to move back toward the terminal area. Small arms fire and grenade explosions came from behind them. The grunts were moving against the heavy machine gun. The sound of grenades, probably 40mm from a M203, caused Tumble to look back. He was watching when a secondary explosion went up, maybe truck gas or ammunition or both or who knows? The grunts had taken care of the nearby shooters or made a lot of noise.

It was a day to be a marine.

"All accounted for, sir. Three wounded and one seriously," Tumble said to C2.

C2 acknowledged and turned his head toward Viking. There, the activity had stopped. Viking was draped with a poncho liner and a blood stain marked where the blood had seeped into the fine, crushed coral below the body. The corpsman stood near the body of the young lieutenant. He was smoking a cigarette. The corpsman noticed the loadmaster with the broken arm bone protruding and the blood running from the arm. He took a drag from his cigarette and ground it out on his boot. As he walked he field stripped the butt with his thumb, put the filter in his pocket and came over to check the man with the broken and twisted and bleeding arm. He looked at Tumble's face, gave Rent a squeeze tube of salve and told him to apply it to Tumble's face. He gave a perfunctory glance at the bloody tee shirt around Tumble's hand and looked in Tumble's eyes for dilation, a sign of shock. Seeing none the corpsman made a triage decision and kept Tumble at the back of his line.

"Captain," said C2. The formality of the title pulled Tumble's attention back to C2. "We have to improve our options. Your Herc is out of the fight and has clobbered a third of the runway, blocked the ramp entrance and the turn-around area. Mine has an RPG hole punched through the vertical stab. My crew is running flight control checks now to see if it is flyable. Your Herc is blocking my access to the runway. We need a piece of heavy equipment to move the wreckage out of the way. If we have to we will fly my Herc out of here."

"What about the 53s?" said Tumble.

"Except for one the others have loaded up and are flying back to Puerto Princesa doing our job. One is coming this way with a last load of grunts from the compound island. It will bring the grunts here, ground refuel, load up as many evacuees as possible and head out. We have evacuees coming out of the woodwork, coming in from town and there is fighting there. We will hold this position and either figure a way to get out on my Herc or hold until the 53s make a round trip. Not reasonable to expect our Hercs to land here. I want you to interview the people we are evacuating and ask specifically if they are aware of any heavy equipment nearby. If we have to go out for it we will coordinate with the grunts. Their CO has a command post set up in a tractor shed the far side of the terminal."

"Doesn't leave much wiggle room," said Tumble.

"No, Captain, it doesn't," said C2 and he smiled. His blue eye and his brown eye sparkled.

"XO, XO," a marine shouted. He was C2's loadmaster and radio operator. He was hanging half out of the port side swing window and pointing at his headset.

C2 turned to his flight engineer and said, "Tell the men one more 53 to ground refuel then break down the rig."

C2 walked toward the crew entrance door of his Herc with the unlit cigar moving in an arc around his mouth as he chewed on the mangled wet tip.

Sporadic small arms fire and the occasional explosion of an RPG or 40mm grenade could be heard in the distance. The benign NEO requiring crowd control had turned into a combat operation. Fortunately, to some extent, the grunts had come prepared for that eventuality. Tumble wasn't sure if they were involved in a revolution or an invasion, not that the definition currently mattered. Not much attention had been paid to this little bit of real estate. The best decision would be to leave and let the locals sort it out.

Tumble walked over to the shade of the terminal where the evacuees were milling about. He called for their attention and asked about the location of heavy equipment nearby. The answer was there was a lot of heavy equipment but none of it was nearby. One evacuee volunteered the location of a small tractor with a landscaper box on the back that was used to dress the coral runway when the tractor could be made to run. Not enough machine to move a burned and still hot Herc but something to start gouging out defensive positions. Tumble sent his young corporal, a north Florida farm boy, with the evacuee to get the tractor.

C2 came out of his Herc and walked over to Tumble. "Plan B," he said. "Wild Bill is a half hour out returning from Thailand. He will take a look at the runway. If he can land he will. All of us, last of the evacuees, grunts, aircrew will pack into Wild Bill's Herc and he will fly us out of here."

Tumble nodded. He did not have a better idea and, in fact, other than waiting for the 53s to make the round trip from Puerto Princesa there was not another idea. The intelligence had missed some points. The strength, armament, and motivation of the bad guys were unknown though, by now, the grunts were working up an idea of the opposition that had been earned the hard way. The whop-whop sound heralded the last inbound 53. It would drop the marine security element from the compound island, refuel, load as many evacuees as possible and head out.

The grunt CO asked C2 to put his marines to work preparing a fallback position. They had come up with a few shovels and rakes and the north Florida boy was working an old Farmall tractor with a landscaper box hanging off the back; improving a shallow benjo ditch that ran on the backside of the terminal either side of the only airport access road. It was a starter for a blocking position. C2 sent Tumble to check on the work progress and he returned to his Herc to keep contact with Wild Bill.

Tumble walked among the aircrew marines checking their slow progress digging in the hard packed dirt with the few shovels and garden rakes they had scrounged. They were digging in the spots a grunt captain had designated. Tumble looked about to envision the fields of fire from the positions. He wished he had paid more attention to the grunt stuff at Quantico's Basic School but he had known he was headed for Pensacola and flight school and had not spent more time than was required on infantry tactics. He did remember that breaking contact with the enemy was a dicey proposition. How to do that and load the last marines, under fire, and get the loaded Herc out of Dodge City was a serious question.

C2 had not entered his Herc. He stood near the nose scanning the sky. A long cord and headset had been run out to him and he was plugged into the UHF radio. The marine in the cockpit stuck his hands out the swing window, all fingers extended, and signaled his hole digging buddies. "Ten minutes out, ten minutes," thought Tumble.

The whop-whop-whop sound of the big inbound CH-53 telegraphed the arrival. Renewed firing could be heard to the east of the runway.

The 53 dropped off the grunt load and began to refuel. Tumble heard Rodeo shouting with the 53 crew chief during the ground refueling.

"How is it on the other island," asked Rodeo.

"All the action is here, gunny," the sergeant crew chief answered. "We won't forget you. We'll be back."

"Thanks, maybe that won't be needed."

The crew chief nodded, completed his duties, signaled the helicopter aircraft commander, the HAC, and packed on more evacuees than the approved 53 load.

The HAC, his 53 loaded and ready, took a heartbeat to give a thumbs up to Tumble then lifted off and gained altitude over the protected area of the runway. He flew east toward Puerto Princesa. Blue collar work the helicopter crews called it.

Rent was walking among the evacuees left at the terminal. He was writing their names on a yellow legal pad and telling them to leave their big bags, bring a toothbrush and a change of clothes. There would not be room for more. Most recognized the required change in the evacuation. It was no longer benign, it was hostile. The protests were minimal.

Tumble was looking west and saw the glint of moving aluminum high and the distinct Herc silhouette visible, maybe 10,000 feet.

"There's Wild Bill," called the marine at the open cockpit swing window.

C2 stood forward of the nose of his Herc, looking up, and talking on the radio. The airborne Herc began a lazy, loose downward spiral overhead the airfield. With his initial altitude cut by half Wild Bill went to about 45 degrees angle of bank and entered his random approach for small arms avoidance. There, green tracer rounds, fainter in the day light, could be seen. The other 12.5 mm was searching for a lucky spot. Wild Bill broke off the approach, leveled and executed a 90 degree timed turn to a 270 degree altitude losing timed turn to set up for a landing toward the wreckage of Tumble's Herc. Neither direction was a good choice. Wild Bill was the only game in town and Wild Bill knew it.

Tumble watched Wild Bill with professional admiration. He walked over and stood with C2.

The grunts were filtered back to their prepared positions. The bad guys were not pressing too hard, probably tough guy amateurs with a few professionals. This wasn't an area like Somalia or Chicago's West Town where the locals participated in daily firefights. They were keeping the grunts busy but too many of them had been killed for the others to press vigorously.

Tumble saw the distinct downward shift in Herc nose attitude when 100 flaps were selected. Wild Bill hit his points and seemed to be in an impact attitude crossing the end of the runway when he tickled the nose up for a slight cushion. The landing impact drove the robust jack screw main landing gear onto the runway surface dissipating energy and killing lift and throwing up smoke like puffs of coral dust around the main tires. The Hamilton Standard props came to max reverse with less than the usual half heart beat safety check for prop spin off at the throttle ground detent. The props and engines roared, the Herc came to a stop and the cloud of fine crushed coral dust enveloped the front half of the Herc. A change in the sound of the prop pitch told that the Herc was out of max reverse and at high speed ground idle.

C2 was talking with Wild Bill on the radio. Tumble turned to look back toward the grunt positions. The intensity of the firing had increased. Breaking contact was looming large. The grunts had come prepared, as always, for a fight, but not a long fight. It was hard to tell if the fire from the grunts was good, disciplined shooting, or they were low on ammo and in a conservation mode.

A change in prop pitch drew Tumble's attention back to Wild Bill's Herc. The Herc taxied forward toward the smoldering remains of his burned Herc, turned sharply toward the side of the runway leaving enough room to straighten the nose wheel. The ramp and aft cargo door opened; a crew member on head set appeared on the open ramp. Tumble watched as Wild Bill, using reverse as needed, did a three point turn on the narrow runway. It was a maneuver he had never seen a Herc perform. The reversed prop blast fanned the embers on Tumble's smoldering Herc to a flare up.

"Captain, get the evacuees moving toward the open ramp on that Herc. It will be an engine running load up," said C2.

"Yes sir," said Tumble. He double timed toward the terminal. He saw a grunt issuing orders and sending a runner off in C2's direction.

The loadmaster with the broken arm still clutched his first aid kit as he began to herd the evacuees. Tumble sent Rent to make a boarding count and Rodeo to keep order as the evacuees loaded. Wild Bill's crew was jamming the evacuees forward in the Herc. They knew there were a lot of people to load. There was no wind and the jet exhaust settled around the open ramp and cargo door.

Glancing toward the access road blocked by the grunt positions Tumble saw a rooster tail of dust. It had to be a vehicle with bad guy reinforcements or a truck with the 12.5 mm machine gun.

Even at ground idle the propellers threw up coral dust and bits of stinging gravel and grit. The odor of the engine exhaust and the sound of the turning props did offer reassurance to those who were ready to go.

Tumble grabbed two of his marines and the young corpsman. They lifted Viking's body draped in a poncho liner marred by congealed blood. There was a primitive scent from the body and deer hunting experience told Tumble that Viking's body cavity had been ripped open. He had not noticed the details of the wounds when they were struggling to get Viking out of the Herc before it blew. They carried Viking's body and put it on the ground just to the side and aft of the ramp. Tumble did not want the body trampled in the final rush to load the Herc. He would see to it that Viking made it aboard.

The grunts increased their firing to form a wall of ball ammo and fire teams here and there left their positions to work toward the waiting Herc. Tumble saw several marines, near simultaneous, pop red smoke. He thought it a masking attempt. He saw before he heard the brush and palms beyond the marine positions part as if cut by a knife and then he heard the tenor zip and the beat of strafing 20 mm cannon. The sound was followed by the rage and roar of a section of F/A-18 Hornets as they flew by low enough to shake coconuts from palm trees. A second section quickly followed. Strafing only, no heavier ordnance, but it would give them the time needed, the time to break contact and load the Herc.

The grunts rose up and began to work their way in coordinated rushes toward the waiting Herc. The Hornets made an air show turn and came back for a second run. Tumble could only imagine the reaction among those on the receiving end but he was sure it involved fear, running for cover, and dying. He did not hear the 12.5 mm. It had been either taken out or the crew was fleeing.

The Hornets attacked, grunts loaded, C2 reached the Herc. "Put Lieutenant Erickson aboard," he said.

Tumble and his marines lifted the body. There was little room as the sardine packed passengers were standing room only. Tumble put his shoulder into the crowd and shoved to get Viking forward of the ramp hinge point then he and the other marines straddled the body to protect it, keep it from being stepped on.

Outside Tumble saw C2 and the grunt CO, a lieutenant colonel, take another look around. The grunt company commander reported to his CO, "Every man accounted for, sir. All aboard," he spoke near and loud to the CO's ear to be heard above the jet noise and whirling props and firing cannon.

The lieutenant colonel sent his captain aboard and turned toward C2. A look of accord passed between them and they boarded, each the last man. They rode the cargo ramp as it closed.

They were leaving the island. Tumble had been under fire. His co-pilot was KIA. He was wounded and he had not laid eyes on an enemy combatant.

The Hornets could be heard making a fourth pass. The Allison T-56 engines drove the Ham Standard props to a deafening roar. The Herc shuttered as Wild Bill stood on the brakes holding them for max power. The brakes were released, there was a millisecond pause and the Herc began to roll then gain speed. At most, Tumble knew, there might be 3,500 feet of runway available for departure. It would be enough. It had to be.

The Herc came sharply off the runway, nose at max effort attitude. They felt slow as they climbed then the nose was eased toward the horizon and the speed increased. Tumble could feel the flaps being milked up in ten degree increments with the speed increase.

The aircraft configuration clean, the Herc crew member near the right paratroop door signaled for C2. C2 jostled past Tumble. He borrowed the right observer's headset and was talking on the intercom system. Two marines wormed their way through, under and over the crowd to report to the grunt CO.

C2 gave a tight smile and pushed the headset back from his left ear while listening to radio chatter with his right. "Stoic Steve, at PAC Fleet, had the Bobby Lee launch the jets at max range."

"Stoic Steve?" said Tumble.

"Admiral Socrates Theophilus, Pacific Fleet, Honolulu. He had to have given the word. The Bobby Lee Hornets launched with drop tanks for max range, no bombs or missiles, needed the stations for fuel. Jettison the drops to decrease the drag as soon as they run dry. They rolled the dice on no air defense and their cannons."

"Worked."

"Yes, it did. We owe the Admiral. A gutsy decision like Admiral Mitscher turning on the fleet lights at the Battle of the Philippine Sea. Success breeds forgiveness so if this turns out good, in the press, the politicians will declare the Admiral a hero. If it doesn't he'll be retired to his Red Neck Riviera home by Easter."

"You know the Admiral?"

"Went to boat school with his youngest brother. I met the future Admiral several times. He came across as someone you could count on."

"You're a ring knocker?"

"Hard to believe, I know."

C2 held up an index finger. He handed the right observer the headset and said, "You have customers. It's time to go to work."

"Wild Bill is bringing the Hornets in for a nip. They are low on fuel and will take what they can get and bingo for Puerto Princesa."

C2 had automatically adjusted his voice to the constant level of noise in the back of the Herc. Tumble did the same and asked, "What was their plan otherwise?"

"Always a bingo profile but with small hope of making it. Prepared to punch out and catch some raft rays waiting for the SAR people to be heroes. Sort of a Jimmy Doolittle Tokyo raid profile."

"I thought so as soon as I saw they were Navy Hornets. We have two Hercs at Puerto Princesa."

"One has low speed drogues for helos. I'll call Wild Bill and remind him. He can coordinate the launch of the high speed drogue Herc for a safety tanker. Sailor Mann is flying that one."

Tumble peered past the right paratroop door observer. He was very aware of the pain in his right hand, his face was burning as if from a very bad day at the beach. He did not feel well. He forced himself to watch the Hornet refuel, keep his mind occupied. Ignore the dead man, a squadron mate, a friend, lying at his feet and ignore the pain. He had paid a small price. There was nothing else to be done. People were packed as thick as those in the Black

Hole of Calcutta. He did see the corpsman climbing the interior side of the Herc, balancing on shoulders with helping hands and working his way forward. The word had been passed that his medical skills were needed. In combat the arrival of a corpsman was greeted with the same thanks as a Johns Hopkins trained surgeon back in the world.

Chapter Seventeen Dognapping

Tumble picked at a flaky bit of dried, scaly skin on his right cheek. He scratched the nub where his little finger had been. It seemed to itch a lot but he had been told that was normal. The Kuwae Naval Hospital surgeons had done a good job cleaning up his hand wound. The burned face had actually been more painful than the lost finger. Don Juan had stabilized the finger and put an ointment on his face at Puerto Princesa, given him some low dose pain meds. He had climbed on a Herc for the return to Okinawa. The DOD had sent in charter flights to pick up the evacuees who were not injured and the Air Force had loaded those judged to need serious medical assistance on a C-17and had flown them to Yokota. Tumble had been offered the opportunity to go to Yokota but had begged off.

All was back to normal, almost. He had worked at his stash job on the Sakura MALLO staff while he waited for the doctors to clear him for discharge. Tomorrow was his last working day in the Marine Corps. Two Herc crews were up from the Rock and he was the honoree at an O Club gathering. It was mid week and not much was happening. Tumble was polite, had a couple of beers and left. It was an awkward party. His friends wanted to see him off in style but they were staying and who knows what Wild Bill would think. Tumble left first. He did not want to spend his last day in the Marine Corps with a hangover.

He was sitting in his BOQ room, lights off, feet propped against the window sill and looking out at the street lights in front of the BOQ when he heard a knock at the door around 0100. He hesitated, turned the desk lamp on, and then opened the door. Bongo stood there with five bottles of beer. He had the four fingers of his left hand stuck into the throat of four of the open, clear glass bottle necks. They dangled, like an aberration of fashion nails, as gold and glass extensions of his fingers. A green, lime island floated beneath each finger. He was drinking from the fifth beer which was held in his right hand.

"Come on in," said Tumble.

"Couple of beers, private party," said Bongo.

"Sure," Tumble said. He took a beer from Bongo's left little finger. There was a lime slice lodged in the neck of the bottle.

"Jewel showed up after you left. I almost didn't come over. Thought she might come here. I listened outside; didn't hear anything."

"She did."

Bongo arched his eyebrows and looked around the room. He noted the packed bags and the made bed.

"I didn't answer the door for her."

"How did you know it was me and not her?"

"The clink of beer bottles."

Bongo took another drink of his beer. He looked at Tumble and remained silent.

"She is a nice girl. I did not want to start something I have no intention of finishing," said Tumble.

They drank beer. Bongo leaning against the desk and Tumble again in his chair. Bongo finished his beer and pursed his lips. Three full bottles of beer still dangled from his left hand. He put the empty bottle on the desk and pulled another beer from the fingers of his left hand. He gestured at Tumble with the two remaining beers. Tumble pulled both from Bongo's fingers, put a full one on the desk and kept one.

"Hard to tell isn't it?" said Tumble.

"Hard to tell?"

"Yeah, am I a good guy or a jerk?"

"Your answer could be different from Jewel's."

"Not if we both took the second choice."

"You're right. By the way C2 also showed up after you left."

"Wild Bill never made it?"

"Who's surprised? Anyway, C2 sends, report to him on the hangar deck at 0600."

"That's five hours from now."

"You can sleep on the jet back to the world. What else have you got to do?"

"Thinking about a night sea wall run."

"Hang on; I'll change and go with you."

Tumble started with a heart pounding thought deprivation pace. The pavement was silver gray in the full moon and splotched with pale yellow from the low-pressure sodium vapor street lights. Bongo, who had been drinking beer since early evening, hung with him. They hit the ramp up to the sea wall and the rough sea swallowed a lot of their moon light. Tumble, looking back for Bongo, fell and skinned his knees and the palms of his hands. Bongo did not falter as Tumble bounced up quickly to deny possible injury. He was not going to sick bay and get held back on his last day.

"You look like you fell in a benjo ditch," said Bongo.

"Not enough beer."

"Only answer."

They were soaked in sweat after the six mile run and Tumble could smell the beer odor mingled with the sweat. They slowed to a walk. Bongo stopped under the street light and looked toward the BOQ.

Tumble could see a lone figure wearing a skirt, arms folded, and standing in the white light of the BOQ portico.

"Don't forget, C2 at 0600 on the hangar deck. Semper fi."

"Semper fi," said Tumble. They shook hands. Bongo walked away.

Tumble walked toward the figure. He knew who it would be.

"Hi."

"Hi. I came to your good bye party."

"I know."

"You weren't there," Jewel said. She paused then said, "Nothing to say?"

"There is nothing to say."

"Ok, what happened in your personal and professional life is not a mystery. Are you going to pitch the rest of your life feeling sorry for yourself in some futile, self punishment gesture?"

"I am thinking about it."

"No, you're not. You're not thinking. We like each other. There is more than a spark of attraction. Don't know where that could go but you don't have enough curiosity or guts to find out."

"That's a statement, not a question."

"Yes it is. I don't know if you are the nice guy I think, an egocentric jerk, or a mental case."

"There are lots of nice guys. Bongo is a nice guy and so are Crusoe and Sailor."

"I do my own choosing."

She was angry and crying hot, angry tears. She beat his chest with her clenched fists.

He took it. He did not hold her. That would be capitulation, commitment, and a mistake. This was best, best for both of them.

Jewel stopped her tears and her assault. She stepped back. Her cheeks were wet with tears, make up smeared, raccoon eyes, her nose was running. Her eyes went cold. She looked at him, pursed her lips, did not say another word, turned and walked away.

Tumble walked up to his second floor BOQ room. He pulled out a bottle of bourbon he had brought to leave as a going away gift for the squadron bar. He cracked the seal and took a short pull. He looked at the bottle, checked the time, decided against it and poured the temptation in the sink.

By 0530 he had showered and was tired of instant coffee. He dressed in his alpha uniform, the greens he liked, and walked to the Officers Club. Breakfast was not served until 0600 but a five dollar bill at the back door of the kitchen would buy a $1.50 cup of early coffee.

The squadron three-plane detachment was working out of the transient hangar. C2 would be there. Tumble had not slept in 24 hours but that was yet to hit him. He had finished the check out procedure and was officially on terminal leave.

The transient hangar was the old style, arched design from the 1950s. It was functional and the shape proclaimed the purpose. Inside and overhead was a network of exposed, steel girders with steel zigzags extending vertical from the primary steel beam and all looked like pieces from a big erector set.

Tumble walked into the hangar and immediately spotted C2 who was standing on the concrete twenty feet into the hangar. He was wearing a drab green flight suit with the sleeves rolled mid forearm. His feet were shoulder width apart, left hand on his hip, coffee cup in his right hand and head tilted back. He was looking into the steel spider web twenty-five feet above the concrete hangar deck.

Tumble followed C2's gaze. He saw a once red and now rust splotched and dinged-up, empty, two pound coffee can hanging from a length of dirty parachute cord. Movement drew his vision right. A marine wearing boots, cammie trousers, and a regulation, green tee shirt was walking, inching his way along the girder, around the zigzag vertical steel supports and toward the suspended coffee can.

"Don't drop my dog," said C2 to the marine.

Across the hangar deck a half a dozen young marines watched the circus act. They seemed to be joking, laughing, smiling, and nervous.

"I paid the ransom, MacFarland. My dog was kidnapped, dognapped. The ransom was paid and they better not drop my dog."

"Yes sir," said Tumble. He was not sure if C2 was serious or joking but it was a serious matter for the marine as he bent to a knee, untied the dog can, pulled the dog up by the leash hand over hand, and cradled it in his arm. He worked his way back to the fixed ladder at the side of the hangar. He climbed down and was met by the crime syndicate. He was their hero. Tumble wondered when and by whom the dog can had been dognapped and suspended.

"Your dog, XO," said the marine.

"Don't make a habit of this. I'll see you and your fellow conspirators on the PT field at 1600."

"You'll bring the beer?"

"A keg, but first I'll run your dicks in the dirt."

"Yes sir."

"Dismissed."

The marines walked away smiling. Now, they were all officially part of the Crazy Cal, the C2 legend. Their story would be told from North Carolina to California, to Arizona, to Japan, to the

Middle East and where ever marines told stories and lies about their legends.

"XO, you wanted to see me?"

"Good thing he did not fall, MacFarland. Your active duty would have been extended. You would have been a witness at the court martial."

"Yes sir," Tumble said. There would have been enough court martial to go around. Knowing the definition of legal culpability was a real spoiler.

"My office. Get yourself a cup of coffee first. Maintenance chief has the best."

Five minutes later Tumble was sitting in front of C2's temporary desk. C2 had his feet up and crossed on one corner and the unzipped lower leg of his flight suit had slid toward his left knee. Exposed was a ragged edged, two inch wide and six inch long scar. It started at the top of his flight boot and went out of sight under the leg of the flight suit. The scar was stretched by additional rounded and raised pink runners of scar tissue radiating from an elliptical, puckered area in the midst of a concave portion of skin and around the puckered area the skin appeared smooth and shiny, without hair or visible pores. The scar made a clear gouge through the thick, black hair on the outside of the calf.

Tumble had noticed C2's leg scar on the PT field. Who had not? It was not a surgical scar. He knew C2 had flown C-130s and helicopters in footnote conflicts around the world which was an easy way to find oneself shot. He did not wear a

Purple Heart medal. It was a wound received in extracurricular activity.

"Do you have any plans after your discharge, Tumble? I don't think the airlines are hiring now. Besides, you wouldn't like that kind of flying, not now anyway, perhaps after you settle down a while. I suggest you think about the reserves, even the inactive. It is a lot easier to get back to active duty if you don't fully break away. Times and situations change. You could be recalled, an option anyway."

"No plans. I thought I would be a career marine, but that didn't work out."

"True, so far. Look at me, though few would consider my career a successful one."

"Yes sir. The CO seems to be doing fine," said Tumble. Not something he should say to the XO but he was on the way out and felt his discipline slip a notch.

C2 had to laugh at Tumble's quick agreement. He sipped his coffee, put his feet on the deck, leaned forward and picked up a yellow number 2 pencil. He tapped the top of the banged up, government issue, gray metal desk, put the pencil down, leaned back and held his coffee cup from a long ago squadron in both hands. He looked out his office window onto the hangar deck. He could see the steel supports where his dog had recently dangled. The faithful dog now lay at his feet. He saw marines going about their morning routine. Then, in soliloquy he said, "Lieutenant

Colonel Hitchcock has been written up for the Navy Cross. He will receive it and he will be a bird colonel. Wild Bill is an asshole not a battlefield coward or an incompetent."

C2 did not give room for Tumble to add a comment. He said, "Tumble, you can always find a flying job. You cannot always find a good flying job. I know a fellow who will give you a lousy flying job for low pay until something better comes along."

"Legal?"

"Far as I know," said C2. Using his right hand, leaving the coffee cup in his left, he unzipped the pocket on the upper left sleeve of his flight suit. He pulled out a folded sheet of paper and handed it to Tumble.

Tumble took the small rectangle of folded paper. He unfolded it to full size. It was a photo copy of a worn business card. Printed on the card was: "Guillermo's Live Stock Flying Service, Miami International Airport, Miami, Florida". The printed phone number was marked through and another was penciled in. There was not an email.

"Tell Guillermo that C2 sent you."

Tumble looked up from the paper.

"They call me Crazy Cal there, too. He will give you a job. It'll keep you afloat. You won't stay long. No one stays long with Guillermo though he does do rehires. There are some apartments geared toward pilots in the Miami Springs area near the airport."

"Thanks, sir. I'll keep this in mind. If I go to Miami I'll give your friend a hello."

"He is a business associate which is different from a friend. Tell the maintenance chief to send the squadron van to the BOQ for your bags."

"Only have two, sir. Don't need a van."

"Tell the maintenance chief to send the squadron van to the BOQ for your bags."

"Yes sir."

"Semper fi, marine.'

"Semper fi."

Made in the USA
Middletown, DE
19 April 2017